ZACH KING

MIRROR
MAGIC

Illustrated by
BEVERLY ARCE

KING

MIRROR
MAGIC

HARPER
An Imprint of HarperCollinsPublishers

ISBN 978-0-06-267724-2

The artist used Adobe Photoshop to create the digital illustrations for this book.
Typography by Joe Merkel
18 19 20 21 22   CG/LSCC   10 9 8 7 6 5 4 3 2 1

First Edition

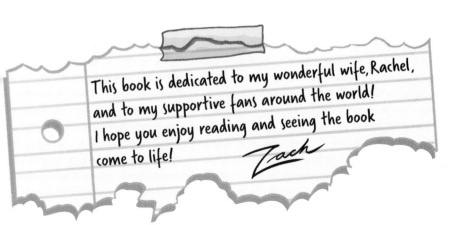

This book is dedicated to my wonderful wife, Rachel, and to my supportive fans around the world! I hope you enjoy reading and seeing the book come to life!

Zach

APP INSTRUCTIONS

Get the AR (Augmented Reality) app
Zach King: Mirror Magic
from zachkingmagic.com on
your mobile device.

Make sure to have enough light.

Point the camera at a
picture in the book to make
the page come to life!

Tap on different
objects to make
magic happen!

ZACH'S KING-DOM

MICHAEL THE CAT

- owned by AARON
- ADORABLE
- Purr-fect in every way!
- Afraid of Heights and Water
- Internet Star!

Principal Riggs

- BALD
- Almost Retired
- Keeps his eyes on ZACH

TRICIA (MEAN)

- likes to get Zach in troubl
- Fashionable
- Wants to be the center o attention

Is there any good in her??

THE ADVENTURE BEGINS. . . .

CHAPTER 1

"Are you sure you don't need help?" Aaron asked.

"Nope," Zach King said confidently. "I got this."

Classes had let out at Horace Greeley Middle School, but Zach and his best friends, Aaron and Rachel, were backstage at the school's brand-new theater and performance space. Needing extra credit, Zach had volunteered to help out on the Drama Club's upcoming production of *Snow White*

and the Seven Dwarves, but he had fallen badly behind painting the sets and backdrops for the play, which was scheduled for Saturday night, only three days away. Zach still needed to paint the Wicked Queen's throne room, the Dwarves' cottage, and the surrounding forest, or the play was going to leave a *lot* to the audience's imagination.

Zach, Aaron, and Rachel faced rows of bare plywood. Rehearsals were taking place on the other side of the unfinished sets, on the stage itself. Zach could hear an indignant voice coming from behind the curtain.

"No, no, no!" protested Tricia Stands, the school's resident queen bee and number one mean girl. Zach couldn't see her from backstage, but he could easily imagine her expression. "I'm the star! I'm Snow White! The spotlight needs to be on *me*!"

"But, Tricia," said the voice of Ms. Flake, the drama teacher, "the audience needs to be able to see the other characters—"

"And this costume isn't nearly princessy enough," Tricia continued, ignoring the teacher. "I'm supposed to be the fairest one of *all*. I need to look fabulous! I can't perform dressed like a peasant!"

Backstage, Aaron rolled his eyes. He squatted on a footlocker full of leftover costumes and stage props, and pushed his mussed hair out of his eyes. His plump gray tabby cat, Michael, sat in his lap and purred obliviously as Aaron petted him. Michael went everywhere with Aaron, even places like school, where he wasn't supposed to be. "I still can't believe Tricia is playing Snow White," he said. "Isn't it obvious that she should be the Wicked Queen?"

"Like she was *ever* going to let anybody else star in the show," Rachel said. "Besides, the Wicked Queen transforms into an ugly old witch in the last act, remember? No way was Tricia going to put on a wig and fake warts."

Personally, Zach thought Rachel should have been Snow White. By yards, she was the prettiest girl in school. She had long brown hair and big dark eyes, and she was smarter than anyone Zach had ever met, not to mention that she held a brown belt in karate and was a champion horseback rider. Today she was dressed for painting, wearing a beat-up T-shirt, jeans, and cowboy boots. She'd come to help Zach, and she'd come ready to get dirty if Zach needed an extra set of hands. Zach knew that even if they had asked her to be in the play, she would rather have been backstage. It was Tricia who always needed to be the center of attention.

"Enough about Tricia," Rachel said, getting back to business. "Let us help you out with the painting. We're here to pitch in."

"Thanks," Zach said. "I appreciate the offer, really, but I can handle this on my own. All I need is . . . magic!"

What most people didn't know, because it was a closely held secret, was that Zach came from a long line of honest-to-goodness magicians, each of whom had their own magic object with its own special power. Everyone in his family could do magic, but for years it had seemed as though Zach had been "skipped," until he'd discovered that he had a unique kind of magic that had its own rules. For one thing, he could use *any* magical object, unlike the rest of his family, who each relied on a single magical object.

Zach pulled a paintbrush out of his backpack. It looked like an ordinary brush, with a polished wooden handle and thick bristles. "I found this in our attic back home.

It belonged to one of my great-great-grandparents, once upon a time, and just wait until you see what it can do!"

Rachel eyed the paintbrush skeptically. "I thought you'd decided to go easy on the magic unless you really needed it."

"And I really need it now," Zach said a bit defensively. "It's the only way to get the sets done in time." Zach knew magic could be tricky sometimes and that, not too long ago, it had gotten him into trouble—but what was the point of *finally* having magic if he couldn't use it to save the day? The show must go on, after all. He popped open a can of forest-green paint. "Trust me, I know what I'm doing."

Aaron groaned and backed away cautiously. "I've heard that before."

"More than once," Rachel added.

Zach scowled, annoyed that his friends didn't seem to think he could manage on his own without their help. "You don't believe me? Get a load of this!"

Principal Riggs stormed off, shaking his head and muttering to himself.

Whew, Zach thought. *That was a close call!*

Principal Riggs didn't know that Zach was really magic. Like most people, he thought that Zach's crazy stunts were just tricks and pranks, and Riggs had a zero-tolerance policy for tricks and pranks and anything else that threatened his ability to retire at the end of the school year. Basically it meant that Zach was by far his least favorite student. Zach didn't mean to cause trouble, of course, but still he seemed to end up in the principal's office—and in detention—again and again.

But not this time. For once, Riggs had not been able to pin the craziness on Zach, despite his suspicions.

"Thank you, magic brushes!" Zach said.

He peeled himself away from the newly painted scenery. Strings of wet paint came away with him. He was going to need a shower and a fresh set of clothes. Maybe he could sneak down to the boys' locker room without anyone noticing?

"Dude, you're a mess," Aaron said.

"Tell me about it." Zach dripped onto the plastic tarp

protecting the floor. "But at least Riggs didn't catch me this time."

Rachel looked over Zach's sloppy self. She sighed and shook her head. "You know, you could have just let us help you instead of using magic."

"But didn't you see what just happened?" Zach collected the paintbrushes and slapped them together, one after another, until they collapsed back into a single brush again. He wiped off the last of the paint and stuffed the brush into his backpack. "Magic saved the day."

"From a mess it created in the first place," Rachel tried to point out.

"Whatever," Zach said. "I know what I'm doing. It's all good."

Rachel shrugged, not wanting to argue. "If you say so."

But she didn't sound like she believed him.

CHAPTER 2

The next day Zach had a dentist's appointment in the morning, and his mom let him take the rest of the school day off afterward. He used his free time to return the magic paintbrush to the attic, where he had found it among all the other old family heirlooms stored there. King family heirlooms were different from most, because many of them were once someone's magical object. To the untrained eye, they looked like random objects—a tennis racket, a snow globe, an hourglass, a pair of scissors, knitting needles, a fishing pole, a top hat, and so on—but each one had once possessed a unique magical ability that could only be activated by the right person. In theory, the objects were powerless now that their original owners had passed away, which was why they were gathering dust in the attic, but Zach knew better. His magic could "ignite" any of the old relics. He just had to figure out what each of them did.

He put the brush back where he'd found it, next to a dusty bowling ball sitting on top of a worn vinyl beanbag chair. Despite the near miss with Principal Riggs, Zach thought yesterday's experiment had worked out okay. The sets *had* gotten painted, after all. So what if things had gone a little haywire? No harm, no foul.

Beats having no magic at all, Zach thought. *Like before.*

"Zach?" a familiar voice called out from downstairs. "Where are you?"

"Up here, Mom," he shouted back.

His mom came up the stairs. Barely five feet tall and

nearly blind without her glasses, she joined Zach in the attic. Her magic ring gleamed on her finger.

"What are you doing up here, honey?" she asked.

Zach couldn't tell her the truth. If his parents knew he had magical powers, they'd insist he be homeschooled like all his cousins and his little sister, Sophie. The only reason he could attend public school with his friends was because his folks still thought he'd been "skipped."

"Um, just looking for something for school . . . for show-and-tell."

He was actually way too old for show-and-tell, but his mom didn't know that. His parents had been homeschooled, too, like all the children in their family, so they were pretty clueless when it came to what public school was like.

"I see."

She glanced around the cluttered attic. Generations of miscellaneous items were piled on top of each other. There was barely space for it all. A rolled-up Persian carpet leaned awkwardly against a department store mannequin that had fallen over onto a quiver of arrows.

A kerosene lantern shared an overloaded shelf with scuba flippers, golf clubs, an antique typewriter, a frying pan, Jell-O molds, and a roll of toilet paper. Zach didn't want to think about what kind of magic that last item was used for.

His mom shook her head. "I keep telling your father that we need to clean up this mess. I'm tempted to have all this old stuff hauled off to the dump." She fiddled with her ring, which had the power to transmute objects from one form to another. "Or maybe I should just turn it all into mist and let it blow out the window."

"No!" Zach said, alarmed. To his mom, the attic's contents were just useless old junk, but to him they were a treasure trove of forgotten magical objects. "You can't do that!"

"Why not?" She looked puzzled by his reaction. "It's junk now. Without their magicians, these are just ordinary . . . things. And they're not doing anyone any good just sitting around here, taking up space."

Zach wished he could tell her the truth. "But . . . they're family heirlooms. They're priceless."

"Like this?" She picked up a deflated rubber inner

tube, followed by a rusty horseshoe. "Or this?"

"Well, maybe not everything," Zach admitted. In fact, he didn't know for sure that *every* item stowed away in the attic had once been magical; some of the junk was probably just . . . junk. "But we can't just chuck it all out without sorting through it first—and saving what's valuable."

His mom eyed him thoughtfully. "Are you volunteering?"

Uh-oh, Zach thought, realizing that he had backed himself into a corner. "Maybe."

"It's settled then," Mrs. King said. "You straighten up the attic. Box up and label whatever you think we should keep, set aside what can be donated to charity, and we'll put the rest out for the trash on Saturday."

Zach couldn't see any way to get out of it. "Okay."

"Thanks, Zach!" She headed downstairs with a smile on her face. "Don't work too hard."

Zach contemplated all the "priceless family heirlooms" that filled the attic. Some of them looked as though they hadn't been touched since before he was born. There was no easy way to tell what was magic and what was junk. Just sorting through all the stuff was going to take days, and then he'd have to pack it all up and stack the boxes neatly enough to satisfy his mom. He groaned at the huge job ahead of him.

What had he gotten himself into?

Zach took out his phone, tempted to ask Aaron and Rachel to come by after school to help him out. Extra hands would lighten the workload in a big way. Plus, the chore would just be more fun with his friends involved. He started to text them, then hesitated.

I have magic now, he remembered. *I can handle this on my own.*

He scanned the attic, searching for inspiration and just the right magic object. An unusual artifact resting atop a sagging wooden bookcase caught his eye. It was a double-lensed magnifying glass consisting of two circular lenses connected by a wooden grip, kind of like the double-bladed light saber used by Darth Manx in *Jedi Kittens I: The Furball Menace.* Zach grinned as a brilliantly sneaky idea occurred to him.

"Yeah," he murmured to himself. "That just might work."

Step One: Standing at the top of the stairs, Zach used his phone to take a picture of the messy attic, which looked like a tornado had picked up a junkyard and tossed it around. He checked to make sure he had the right angle, then scrambled downstairs to his room and fired up his computer.

Step Two: Zach loaded his photo onto the laptop and called it up on the screen. Then he went to work cleaning it up electronically. Working the cursor and keyboard, he deleted most of the clutter from the picture and replaced it with stock photos of neatly stacked moving boxes. He click-and-dragged the boxes over to the walls of the attic to make the room look much tidier than it actually was in real life.

Aaron could do this much faster and easier, Zach thought, remembering how talented his friend was when it came to editing viral videos. Once again, he considered enlisting Aaron's help but decided against it. This was a matter of pride now. He didn't need to go running to his friends every time he got in a jam. *All I need is magic.*

He kept at it, and before long the attic looked perfectly

neat and tidy—onscreen, at least. He took a moment to admire the doctored photo before printing a copy of it.

"That should do it."

Step Three: Printout in hand, Zach ran back up to the attic. Standing at the top of the stairs, he compared the photo to the actual attic in all its messiness. Everything seemed to line up just right.

"Yes! This is going to work."

His plan was to blow up the photo to life size and hang it from the ceiling so that it looked as though the attic was clean from the top of the stairs. Nobody ever came up here anyway, so the optical illusion should be good enough to fool his mom—and save Zach hours of tedious stacking and packing.

Now he just needed to enlarge the photo, which is where the magic magnifying glass came in. He placed the photo on the floor and picked up the magnifying glass by its handle. He aimed the top lens at the photo—which instantly shrank to the size of a postage stamp.

"Oops!" he blurted. "Wrong way!"

He realized that the object was a combination

magnifying-reducing glass, with a convex lens on one end of the handle and a concave lens at the other. He spun the handle around so that the magnifying lens was pointed at the now teeny-tiny photo, which immediately regained its original size and kept on growing until it was large enough to stretch across the entire attic. Zach put down the magnifying glass before the picture got too big.

Step Four: In order to hang the photo from the ceiling, Zach grabbed a stapler and brought it upstairs with him. But the ceiling was high above his head. He needed to stand on something if he was going to reach it. Glancing around the attic, he spotted a stool resting in front of a standing, fancy, oval-shaped mirror. He grabbed the stool and placed it beneath one end of a long wooden rafter crossing the ceiling in just the right place.

That should get me high enough, Zach hoped. *Maybe.*

Holding on to a corner of the giant photo with one hand and clutching the stapler with the other, he clambered up onto the stool, which was a lot more rickety than he expected. It wobbled unsteadily beneath him as he stretched and strained to reach the rafter, but

Step 1

Take a picture of the messy attic

Step 2

Edit the picture to make the room look clean

Step 3

Make the new picture big with a magic magnifying glass

Step 4

Hang the new picture!

Zach refused to give up, even though the bottom of the wooden beam was still just out of reach.

Maybe if he leaned out just a little bit farther . . .

Too far!

The stool toppled out from beneath him. Losing his balance, Zach fell toward the large standing mirror. He saw his own frantic expression in the mirror as he braced himself for impact. He winced in anticipation.

This was going to suck!

But instead of crashing into the mirror, he *passed through it.*

CHAPTER 3

Instead of smashing into the glass mirror, Zach crashed into the floor. He sat up and checked to make sure he was still in one piece. He shook his head to clear it. Dazed, he took a moment to realize that he wasn't in the attic anymore.

Wait a second. . . .

Looking around in confusion, he was surprised to find himself back at school, on the stage where the *Snow White* rehearsal had been going on yesterday. The theater was empty at the moment, so Zach had the stage to himself, but he heard voices and activity in the halls outside. He recognized the familiar background noise of kids heading to and from their classes.

Zach scrambled to his feet and tried to figure out what had happened. Had he knocked himself out falling from the stool? Did he have a concussion? Was he dreaming? He pinched himself—hard—and yelped out loud.

Nope, definitely not a dream.

He suddenly noticed the antique wooden mirror on the stage behind him. Instead of being tucked away in the attic, it was now part of the set, as though it had somehow been drafted into duty as the Wicked Queen's Magic Mirror. Zach's baffled expression was reflected in the glass, which was still intact despite Zach falling into it.

Zach didn't understand. He'd occasionally fallen through solid objects before, just by accident, but he'd seldom ended up somewhere else. The only time he'd ever traveled from one place to another by magic was when he'd used a pair of magical snapbacks, but those had been eaten by a crocodile months ago. Was transporting him to school the mirror's magic power?

A bell rang, signaling that it was time for students to

head to their next class. Unsure what else to do, Zach exited the theater and joined the throngs of students making their way through the halls of the school. Lockers and inspirational posters lined the corridor.

Zach still felt a little groggy from his collision with the floor, so he decided to dart into the boys' room to splash some cold water on his face. His head still smarted, too, so it couldn't hurt to check himself in the mirror, just in case he was bruised or swelling up.

But when he turned left into the boys' room, he was suddenly greeted by shouts and shrieks from a row of girls lined up at the sinks. They hurled wads of wet paper towels at him.

"What are you doing here!"

"Get out!"

"This is the girls' room, you creep!"

Blushing in embarrassment, Zach beat a hasty escape while stammering apologies. "Sorry! Just got mixed up! Sorry!"

But how had he gotten mixed up? As Zach retreated back into the hall, he stopped to orient himself but couldn't figure out how he had gotten so spun around. It didn't make any sense. The boys' room had *always* been on the left before. It was almost as though everything was reversed now. . . .

Reversed.

Zach froze as the pieces came together in his brain. School was the same, except that it wasn't. Left was right. Right was left. Everything was backward—like on the other side of a mirror.

He really had fallen through the magic mirror into some kind of Reverse World!

His eyes scanned his surroundings. Everything looked more or less the same as he remembered.

Kids channeled past him on their way to class. He recognized most of them, or thought he did, so maybe everything wasn't as different as he feared. He gasped in relief as he spotted Rachel coming toward him, clutching an armload of books to her chest. Her eyes were turned down toward the floor.

"Rachel!" He rushed toward her, happy to see a familiar face. "Boy, am I glad to see you!"

She paused and looked up at him, a puzzled expression on her face. "Excuse me?"

"Just wait until you hear what's happening. You're not going to believe it!"

"My name is Raquel," she said, eyeing him warily. "Can I help you?"

Raquel? Zach looked more closely at the girl in front of him. She was dressed in a turtleneck and a wool skirt. She seemed shy, like she was afraid to even look Zach in the eye. "Whoa. Whoa. Wait a second. Let me get this straight. You're not the real Rachel? My Rachel?"

"I'm Raquel, and we've barely met. You're freaking me out." Raquel backed away from him like she thought he had gone crazy or something. "I don't want to be late to class, so I'll just be going—"

"Wait, please!" Zach panicked at the thought of being left alone in Reverse World. He grabbed her arm to keep her from departing. "You don't understand. This is all backward!"

"Let go of me!"

A blast of magical energy hit Zach like a shock wave, knocking him off his feet and sending him skidding backward down the hall on his butt. Startled kids dived out of the way to avoid being crashed into before Zach slammed into a trophy case at the end of the hall. Sports trophies and other awards rattled on their shelves as the back of Zach's head banged into the glass display case.

"Oh no!" Raquel looked mortified. "I'm sorry. I didn't mean to do that, I promise!" All eyes turned toward her, and she fled from the scrutiny, disappearing around a corner. "Gotta go!"

Zach blinked in surprise. He didn't know what shocked him more: the blast or that Rachel—that is, *Raquel*—had magic in this world.

Could things get any weirder?

"Oh, Jak! Are you okay?"

It took Zach a minute to realize that somebody was talking to him. *Jak? Oh, that's me.*

"Jak, can you hear me? Are you okay?"

To his surprise, Tricia, of all people, came rushing toward him. Like Raquel, she looked different on this side of the mirror. Back home, Tricia was a middle school fashionista who only wore the latest designer clothes and whose long, blond hair was always stylishly groomed. But this Tricia had her hair drawn back in a ponytail and was wearing a baggy sweater that had

"Save the Whales" printed on the front. Even stranger, she looked genuinely concerned about Zach's well-being.

"Tricia?" he said hesitantly.

"Trina." She gave him a worried look. "I hope you don't have a concussion."

"I don't think so." Zach rubbed the back of his head. He felt a goose egg where his head had smacked into the trophy case. "Just a bit of bump, that's all."

"Well, let me take care of that right away." Trina pulled a fluffy, pink mitten out of her pocket and slipped it onto her hand. "What's the good of having healing magic if you can't help out your fellow classmates?"

Before Zach knew what was happening, she'd applied the mitten to the back of his head. He felt a tingling sensation as the bump shrank away. Trina's healing touch made his head feel better but left him more confused than ever.

"Hang on. You have magic, too?" He suddenly realized that everyone was looking at them. He lowered his voice to a whisper. "Should you be doing that in public?"

"Why not? It's no secret," she replied. "This is Horace Greeley Magic School, after all."

Magic school?

Zach tried to process that. Glancing around, he suddenly noticed odd little details he'd overlooked before. A taped-up poster hyped an upcoming flying-carpet race, while another poster urged kids to join the school's Crystal Ball Club. A thirsty kid pulled a steaming cup of hot chocolate out of his back pocket. A drop of soapy water landed on his head and he looked up to see the school janitor, Mr. McGillicuddy, defying gravity while casually scrubbing the ceiling with a damp sponge. Zach stepped back to avoid being dripped on again.

"So everyone has magic here?" he asked.

"Well, most everyone," she said gently, as though she was worried about hurting his feelings. "But you know, Jak, that nobody thinks any the less of you just because magic skipped you over. We're all special in our own way."

By now, Zach had picked up on the fact that he was called "Jak" here. He assumed that Jak must be a Reverse World version of himself, and that he must be somewhere around here. It seemed like Jak was the only kid in school without any sort of magical object or power. It didn't take much for Zach to realize that being Jak must be the pits.

But the fact that magic was routine here changed everything for Zach, since it meant that maybe he didn't have to hide what had happened with the magic mirror. He was used to covering up any magical mix-ups to protect his family's secret, but if everybody here already believed in magic, then maybe he could just explain the situation.

"Look, this may sound crazy—or not—but suppose I told you that I fell through a magic mirror earlier . . ."

Trina's eyes widened in shock. "Don't even joke about that! You know that mirror magic is strictly forbidden. Suppose one of the teachers heard you and thought you were serious!" She gently felt the back of his head to make sure the bump was gone. "Maybe you got hit harder than I thought."

"Forbidden?" Zach asked.

"Of course. You can't have people going back and

forth between worlds willy-nilly. Magic mirrors have been banned for ages, ever since those Backward folks caused all that trouble in the fifties. You know that, Jak."

Zach had no idea what she was referring to, but he got the message. Messing with magic mirrors could land you in serious trouble here. He was about to ask her more about it when a shadow fell over Zach. He looked up to see Principal Riggs looming over him, gazing down at him as Zach backed against the lockers.

"What's going on here?" the principal asked.

Zach gulped. This Mr. Riggs looked different from the one he knew. He had a full head of hair, for one thing, and he was wearing a bow tie and was missing his bushy mustache. But Zach still felt an all-too-familiar sense of apprehension. Some things, it seemed, never changed, no matter what side of the mirror you were on. He was in trouble again. He wondered if the principal's office was at the other end of the school in Reverse World. He suspected he was about to find out.

"Jak just had a little spill, Principal Ruggs," Trina explained. She took off her magic mitten and tucked it back in her pocket. "I healed his bump, but he still seems disoriented. I think maybe he should go to the infirmary."

Mr. Ruggs, not Mr. Riggs, Zach noted. He also observed that Trina didn't tattle on Raquel, which his Tricia would have done in a heartbeat. He was starting to lose track of all the differences between Reverse World and home. It was a lot to take in.

"Oh dear," the principal said, sounding way more sympathetic than upset. "Let me give you a hand, Jak." He reached down to stand Zach up straight. "Maybe you *should* see the nurse. Can't be too careful with my favorite student."

Zach's jaw dropped. This was just too much.

"Nah, I'm fine," he insisted, deciding to play it cool. After what Trina had just said about mirror magic being against the rules, it was probably safer to pretend that everything was normal, just like he usually did when things got weird and magical back home. "No need to worry about me."

"Are you sure, Jak?" Ruggs placed a reassuring hand on Zach's shoulder. "I know it's not easy coping without magic, but remember, my door is always open if you need someone to talk to."

Zach had trouble hiding his confusion. A friendly principal who was looking out for him was even more bizarre than a Tricia who wanted to save the whales and take care of people. Zach tried to crack a joke to cover how weirded out he was.

"Until you retire, of course."

"Retire?" Principal Ruggs echoed, then laughed out loud. "Good one, Jak! Glad to see your sense of humor is still intact." He chortled at the very notion of retiring. "You know me. I love my job. They'll have to drag me out of here!"

Zach couldn't believe his ears. Back home, Mr. Riggs was counting the days until he retired, but here . . .

Yep, Zach thought. *This is Reverse World, all right.*

"But seriously, Jak," Ruggs said, "feel free to take the rest of the day off if you need some time to recuperate. Shall I call your folks to come pick you up?"

"No!" Zach blurted. He wasn't ready to cope with a reversed version of his family just yet. Everything was

already too strange and different; he needed time to get the lay of the land and to figure out how to get back where he belonged. "I don't want to miss out on any classes, I mean."

"Now *that's* the Jak Kong I remember," Ruggs said. "The perfect student." He slapped Zach on the back as he strolled away, beaming warmly at all the kids crowding the hall. "Keep up the good work!"

Trina stayed behind with Zach. She placed a hand on his forehead to see if he had a fever. "Are you sure you're okay, Jak?"

Zach couldn't get used to this new, more humanitarian version of Tricia, but he already liked her better than the genuine article. "I'll be all right, really. Thanks for not squealing on Rach . . . *Raquel*, by the way. That was nice of you."

Trina shrugged. "It's not her fault that she can't control her own magic. No wonder she's so afraid of her powers."

Raquel afraid? This Reverse World kept on surprising Zach. His Rachel had once wrestled an alligator without hesitating. Zach was there. He saw her do it. So he found it hard to imagine any version of Rachel being afraid of anything.

"Gotta scoot," Trina said. "See you around." She started away from him, then glanced back at him over her shoulder. "I like what you've done with your hair, by the way."

"My hair?"

Zach wondered what Jak's hair looked like.

Come to think of it, where was the real Jak, anyway?

CHAPTER 4

EARLIER:

Jak grunted as he lugged the heavy wooden mirror onto the stage. He'd found it in his parents' basement and decided to donate it to the Drama Club's upcoming production of *Snow White* to score some brownie points at school. The way he saw it, the antique mirror was a lot more impressive than the junky "Magic Mirror" the club had been planning to use.

Too bad there was nobody on hand to help him cart the mirror around or to use their magic to make the chore easier. Not for the first time, he resented the fact that he had been skipped over, magic-wise.

If I had magic like everyone else, he thought crankily, *I could just levitate this darn mirror, or teleport it, or pull it out of a hat, or shrink it down to pocket size, or something cool like that.*

Straining and sweating, he wrestled the mirror into place on the stage. His grip slipped, however, and the solid wooden frame landed on his foot.

"Ouch!" He hopped around, wincing. "Stupid, heavy mirror!"

A throbbing toe didn't help his bad mood. Losing his temper, he threw a punch at the mirror—*and fell through the glass and landed in . . .*

His attic?

Jak didn't understand. A minute ago he was on the stage at school, and now he was back home in his attic, which had somehow become completely cluttered with junk. He barely recognized the place, it was so crowded, despite the fact that his mom had converted the attic into a craft room years ago. What was going on?

The mirror was nowhere to be seen, although an

overturned stool was lying on the floor over by the stairs, along with a huge, mural-size photo of the messy attic. Jak couldn't begin to guess what that was all about.

Not that it really mattered. Despite his confusion, Jak was suddenly hit with a thrilling possibility: Had he actually just done magic?

Or had the mirror simply worked its magic on him?

He gulped at the prospect. Magic mirrors were strictly illegal, which was why an ordinary mirror was being used in the play. But maybe his family's old mirror was actually magic after all, and nobody had ever realized this before. He wasn't sure how he'd activated it without magic, or if it had activated itself somehow. And why had it transported him from the school to the attic?

"Honey?" his mom's voice called from downstairs. Her voice sounded slightly different, but he still recognized it. "Are you still sorting through all those old magic objects? Do you need more boxes? I'm heading out to the store in a few, so let me know."

Magic objects? Jak gaped at the huge collection of random junk, which was suddenly a lot more interesting.

When and why had his family started hoarding magic objects? Nobody in the Kong family had magic; it was their family curse.

"What magic objects?"

"Very funny," his mom said. "The ones you promised to sort through, remember?"

Jak didn't remember that at all, but he was always forgetting about his chores, so he automatically acted like he was on top of things, just out of force of habit.

"It's okay, Mom. I think I'm good for now."

"Okay," his mom replied. "Thanks again for tackling this job, especially on your day off."

What day off? Jak wondered. He pretended he knew what she was talking about. "No problem, Mom."

Jak surveyed the cluttered attic, wondering what magic might be hiding in plain sight all around him. Curiosity drew him to an old wooden wardrobe. He wondered if this was where those mysterious "magical objects" were.

He approached the wardrobe and tugged on the door, which stubbornly resisted him at first. Grunting, he tugged on the stuck door until it finally swung open to reveal a long, dark tunnel leading to . . . where?

It's a portal, he realized. Jak had learned something about magical portals at school, even if he could never operate one himself. He wished he had paid more attention to those lessons in class. Thinking of school reminded him that, despite what his mom had said about a "day off," it was still a school day as far as Jak knew. He was supposed to be in class right now.

"Yikes," he said aloud. "I need to get back to school!"

All at once, a powerful suction grabbed onto Jak, tugging him through the portal. He suddenly found himself inside his school locker, crammed in with textbooks, school supplies, and what smelled like a leftover egg sandwich. Light filtered through a metal grate in the locker door, allowing him to glimpse the hallway beyond. He tried the door but found it locked from the outside.

Uh-oh. Did I do that?

Spinning around in the tight space, which wasn't easy, Jak tried to go back the way he came, but he smacked into the back of the locker instead. He pushed against it, trying to reopen the portal, but it didn't budge. He was trapped inside with no way out. Who knew magic portals could be so inconvenient?

"Hey!" he shouted, banging on the locker door. "Somebody get me out of here!"

Through the grate, he saw kids stop and stare at the commotion. Nobody seemed to know what to do until a girl pushed through the crowd to get to the locker. It took Jak a second to recognize her.

"Raquel?"

"Hang on, Zach," she said. Jak was a little weirded out that she'd gotten his name wrong. "I'll get you right out of there."

Jak had no idea how she knew his combination, but she quickly unlocked the door and he tumbled out into the hall. He took a deep breath and stretched his limbs. It felt good to be free.

"Thanks, Raquel!"

"*Rachel*," she corrected him before turning toward the gaping spectators. "Nothing to see here. Move it along."

She leaned in to whisper to Jak. "What was that all about? How did you end up in your locker? Were you messing with your magic again? Good thing I happened to be nearby."

Jak didn't follow any of that. "My magic? And how come you knew my locker combination? Or did you use magic to open it?"

"Since when do I have magic?" she replied. "We traded combinations forever ago—like friends do. You get enough air in there? You're not making any sense."

"Wait," Jak said, trying to keep up. "Did you just say

I can do magic?"

"So what else is new?" Rachel shrugged, oddly unimpressed. "Just keep your voice down. You want the whole school to find out?"

"Why not?" he asked.

"Because it's top secret, of course. What's up with you?" She eyed him quizzically. "And what on earth did you do with your hair?"

"My hair?" He reached up to check it but was distracted by the sight of Trina, who looked very different from the friendly healer he knew. Jak couldn't take his eyes off the pretty blond girl heading toward them, sipping on a strawberry frappé. She was much more stylishly dressed than usual and flaunting long, lustrous yellow hair. An entourage of other girls her age accompanied her, but she definitely stood out from the pack. "Whoa!" he blurted, his eyes bugging out. "Is that really Trina? When did she get so cool?"

"Is that so?" Rachel said frostily. She gave him a dirty look before she scowled and stormed away. "See you later, Zach—after you come to your senses."

What was that all about? Jak scratched his head. She

was acting like she was his best friend when he barely knew Raquel at all. Shrugging, he headed toward Trina to see if she would give him some of her healing magic for his toe. It was still throbbing from when he'd dropped the mirror on it. Trina was always ready to use her magic mitten on anyone who needed it. She had the biggest heart in school.

"Hey, Trina! Looking good! Would you mind—"

"Zach King! You weirdo!"

She hurled the frappé into his face. The cold, sugary concoction splattered all over him as he gasped in shock.

"*That's* for your sneaky paint trick yesterday!" she snarled. "And my name is Tricia, you moron!"

Zach sputtered through the frappé all over his face. It ran down onto his shirt. "What are you talking about?"

"Don't play dumb with me!" she spit. "We both know that was one of your stupid magic tricks!"

"Magic tricks?" he said excitedly as the truth sank in. "I actually did magic tricks?"

Trina glared at him. "You don't need to sound so happy about it, you freak!"

She shoved past him, bumping him with her shoulder.

Her entourage tagged along with her, laughing and smirking at Jak, who just stood there, looking like a sticky, gloppy mess, but more excited than ever. It sucked that Trina had gotten so mean, but who cared about that? The important thing was that he could actually do magic at last—just like with the wardrobe in the attic.

The flung frappé was soaking through his shirt. Needing to clean up, he turned right into the boys' room—or what he thought was the boys' room.

Screams and shouts chased him out of the girls' room, and as he ran back into the hall, he bumped right into a looming figure who looked disturbed by the commotion.

"Mr. Ruggs!" Jak said, relieved to see the friendly principal. He took a closer look and blinked in surprise. "Where did all your hair go?"

The principal, who was now bald and sporting a bushy mustache, scowled at Jak. He put his hands on his hips. "What did you just say?"

"Sorry," Jak said with a shrug. "You just caught me off guard." He couldn't wait to tell Ruggs the big news. "Guess what? I can do magic now, just like every—"

"That's enough, Zach King! Barging into the girls'

restroom, raising a ruckus, is just another magic trick too? For your juvenile videos?" His harsh tone sounded nothing like him. He grabbed Jak by the ear and started dragging him down the hall. "My office . . . *now*."

"But . . . didn't you hear me? I've got magic now! I'm not skipped over anymore!"

"You won't be skipping anything ever again, if I have anything to say about it," the principal said, misunderstanding. "And no more talk of magic. I've had quite enough of your disruptive parlor tricks, Zach King!"

"No, no," Jak said, trying to explain. "I'm talking about real magic!"

"Don't be ridiculous!" the principal scoffed. "There's no such thing. I don't know what you're trying to pull here, but . . ."

He kept talking, but Jak stopped listening as the pieces finally came together in his mind. The changed names, the way everything was so different . . . this wasn't his world at all. He hadn't just transported from the school to the attic and back again. He'd fallen through a forgotten magic mirror into some sort of parallel world that was the opposite of the one he was used to.

A world where nobody else had magic, but he did.

He should have been freaked out, but instead a grin stretched across his face.

Oh boy, he thought, *this is going to be fun! So long as I can keep passing as this Zach kid, I can be magic. I'm never going back!*

CHAPTER 5

REVERSE WORLD

"And that's how we discovered that magic was one of the fundamental forces of the universe, along with gravity and electromagnetism," the science teacher informed Zach and the rest of the class. Mathematical equations mixed with magical symbols on the blackboard behind him. "After lunch, we'll do some magic training exercises and lab work." He looked at Zach. "You're excused from those lessons, Jak, as usual."

The bell rang, dismissing the class.

It was lunch hour, and though Zach had managed to pass as "Jak" for a class or two, he was getting anxious to return to his own world. He didn't want to think about what would happen if his mother had the mirror in the attic hauled off to the garbage dump on Saturday as she planned. So instead of heading to the cafeteria, Zach was sneaking to the school theater when a familiar voice called out.

"Dude, where you going? The cafeteria's this way."

Zach turned toward the voice, not sure what to expect. "Aaron?"

"Baron," said a kid who looked like he could be Aaron's superbuff twin brother. Baron's hair was neatly styled and he was wearing an athletic jersey. People high-fived him as he approached Zach. "What's the matter, Jak? Forget my name? I heard you got a bump on the head earlier, but I didn't think it was *that* bad."

Zach tried to cover up his lapse. "Still a little foggy, I guess."

"Nothing a healthy meal can't fix," Baron said, steering Zach toward the cafeteria instead of the theater. "I don't know about you, but I could really dig into a nice, big ol' salad right now."

Zach glanced back over his shoulder toward the theater. He wished he could explain about the magic mirror, but that could get both him and Jak in trouble, so Zach decided to play along for now. The magic mirror on the stage would have to wait until he could get to it without attracting any unwanted attention.

And besides, he was kind of hungry. Maybe he shouldn't try jumping from one world to another on an empty stomach.

"Sounds good," Zach agreed, "but . . . a salad? Really?"

"You know me, dude. I'm all about being healthy and exercising."

Zach would have choked if he'd been drinking something. Baron was nothing like Aaron so far. Zach wondered if they had anything in common.

"And cats?"

"More of a dog person, really." He gave Zach some serious side-eye. He tugged on a chain around his neck to reveal a thin metal dog whistle. "You know that, Jak."

"Right, sure," Zach said, laughing it off. "I'm just messing with you."

He was dying to know what kind of magic Baron had in Reverse World, but he couldn't think of a sneaky way to ask without revealing that he'd come through a magic mirror. *Guess I'll find out soon enough,* he thought, *if I don't get back through the mirror first.*

Baron exchanged high fives and funny greetings with more kids as they entered the cafeteria. Zach spotted Raquel sitting by herself in a corner and started toward her, but Baron called him back.

"Dude, our table is over here, remember?" Baron shook his head. "Boy, you are spacy. You may really want to see a doctor today."

"Ha," Zach said. "No worries. I'm cool."

Baron guided him toward a crowded table full of cool kids who scooted aside to make room for them. Zach felt bad about turning away from Raquel, but he reminded himself that she wasn't his Rachel and that this wasn't his world. With any luck, he'd be back with his real friends before long.

What went on in Reverse World was not his problem.

After dropping off their backpacks at the table, Zach and Baron got in line for some chow. Sure enough, Baron hit the salad bar for a huge plate of leafy greens, while Zach helped himself to a soda and a slice of cheese pizza, which tasted like greasy cardboard—just like the pizza at his real school. Apparently cafeteria food was the same in every dimension. In a weird way, Zach found that kind of reassuring.

"So, we still on for shooting a new video this weekend?"

"Sure, I guess," Zach said. "A magic video?"

Back where he came from, Zach had his own YouTube channel, where he posted videos of him performing amazing magical feats. Most people assumed it was all special effects and stage magic, but Aaron knew the truth. He was the one who filmed the magic tricks for Zach and made them look their best.

"Are you serious?" Baron scoffed. "Anybody can do magic—no offense, dude—but cute dog tricks are my whole brand. That's what goes viral and racks up tons of likes."

"Well, sure, of course," Zach muttered. "That makes perfect sense."

No wonder Baron is so popular here, he realized. *He's the video star, not me.*

Zach tried not to let that bother him.

"You know it!" Baron slapped Zach on the back. "And I can't do it without my faithful photographer. You're my main man, assuming your head is still in the game?"

"Count on it," Zach said, speaking for Jak.

With any luck, he'd be back in his own world long before then!

Lunchtime seemed to last forever as Zach did his best to avoid giving himself away. Fortunately, Baron was the center of attention, so nobody was paying much mind to Zach. He wondered how the real Jak felt about that.

By now, Zach had figured that he and Jak had traded places, since the real Jak was nowhere to be seen. Zach figured there was only one place the missing Jak could be—on the other side of the mirror.

A voice called from across the cafeteria. "Hey, Baron, my man! Incoming!"

Zach looked up to see a paper plate spinning through the air like a Frisbee. He wondered what was up, but Baron laughed as he jumped to his feet and blew on

his dog whistle. The sound was too high-pitched for humans to hear, but that wasn't the surprising part. Baron started running, and in midstride he magically turned into a black-and-white border collie. He leaped into the air in time to catch the flying plate in his jaws.

A second later, Baron turned back into a human as he landed with the plate in his mouth.

"Good catch, man!" a student congratulated him.

Baron spit the plate into a nearby trash bin. "What can I say? It's a gift."

More of a dog person, really, Zach remembered Baron saying before. *Guess I know now what his magic whistle does.*

Zach was still processing that when the bell finally rang and lunch ended.

"Later, dude," Baron said as he took a big swig from a fresh bottle of mineral water. He washed it around his mouth, gargled, and spat it out into the water fountain before looking over at Zach. "I never get used to the taste of dog mouth. Hardest part of turning back human. Hey—what's my name again?"

"Baron," Zach answered.

"That's more like it." Baron grinned as he wandered off with the other kids. "See, you just needed a little food in your stomach. You're as right as rain."

Zach sighed as Baron and the others headed off to class without him. He headed out with them until Baron reminded him that he had a free study period now, while they were taking magic class. Zach took the opportunity to slip back into the theater to try to go back through the mirror. Quietly, he climbed onto the stage, where the magic mirror waited for him. He glanced around to make sure nobody was looking. It wouldn't make any difference to him, of course, once he got back home, but he didn't want to make trouble for Jak, when he came back. Zach really hoped his double was being just as thoughtful in the "real" world.

One thing at a time, Zach thought. First, he had to get back where he belonged. *Then* he could worry about what had happened while he was away.

Zach peered at the mirror. He half expected to see Jak staring back at him, but he saw only his own reflection instead. He reached for the mirror, hoping that his hand would pass effortlessly through the glass.

Nope.

The glass was just as solid as it appeared, leaving Zach stumped. As far he knew, he hadn't done anything special to activate the mirror back in the attic. He had just fallen straight through it. Zach didn't see any choice; he just needed to go for it.

Voices sounded outside in the hall. He couldn't hesitate any longer. He had to take the chance while he had it.

"Here goes nothing," he muttered.

Crossing his fingers for luck, he backed up to get a running start, then dived headfirst into the mirror.

CRASH!

Zach bounced back onto his butt. He gasped in dismay as the mirror cracked right down the middle, splitting his reflection in two.

"Oh no!" he blurted. "I broke it!"

But that wasn't the worst part. He was still on the stage, which meant that he was still stuck in Reverse World. The awful truth hit him like a pie to the face. He couldn't make the mirror work because he didn't have magic in this world. He was stuck unless Jak reopened the doorway from the other side.

"Did you hear that?" a voice said right outside the door. "What was that crashing noise?"

"I don't know, Ms. Fluke," a student answered.

Uh-oh, Zach thought.

He scrambled to his feet. He had enough to deal with right now. The last thing he needed was to get busted for cracking the mirror, especially since he couldn't explain about it being magic without getting into serious hot water. Moving quickly, he ducked backstage and hid behind the scenery as he heard the theater door swing open.

"Oh dear!" the drama teacher exclaimed. "What happened to our mirror?"

"It's just a crack, Ms. Fluke," a kid in the Drama Club said. "Maybe we can still use it in the play?"

"Maybe," Ms. Fluke agreed, "though I feel bad for whoever broke it. Seven years of bad luck and all. . . ."

Ms. Fluke went back to preparing for the play, and Zach snuck out the back door of the theater into the parking lot behind the school, where it immediately started to rain . . . hard. Caught in an unexpected downpour, Zach dashed around the side of the school, looking for cover, only to slip and fall in a mud puddle.

Just my luck, he thought, wiping off his muddy hands on his muddy pants.

And then a horrible thought struck him: What if, in this world, breaking a magic mirror *really* meant seven years of bad luck?

Cold and wet, Zach had no idea what to do about it. He was stuck in Reverse World; time was running out.

For all he knew, the mirror back home was still going to be carted off to the dump on Saturday. If it got buried in a landfill, or smashed to pieces in a trash compactor, he might never see his real friends and family again!

CHAPTER 6

Jak tried not
to gape as Zach's
mom fixed dinner—
using magic!

Mrs. King looked just like Jak's mom, except that she wore glasses and a magic ring. As Jak helped set the kitchen table for dinner, he watched in wonder as Mrs. King dumped some uncooked noodles, meat, and tomato sauce in a pan on the stove. The ring sparkled briefly and, right before Jak's eyes, the raw ingredients transformed into hot lasagna that smelled delicious. His stomach grumbled loudly.

"Sounds like somebody's hungry," Mrs. King said.

"You bet . . . Mom," Jak said. She looked so much like his real mom, except that his real mom had curly hair, blue eyes, and a hint of a Southern accent. He sat down at the table. "That smells fantastic!"

She gave him a puzzled look. "Just my usual recipe," she said, as though it was nothing to be excited about. Jak hoped he hadn't already blown his cover, but Mrs. King let it go. "Do me a favor, dear, and tell your dad and sister that dinner is ready."

"Save your breath." A childish voice came out of nowhere, startling Jak. He glanced around but couldn't see anybody except Mrs. King. "Here I am."

The air shimmered, and a nine-year-old girl suddenly appeared by the table, sporting a pair of hot-pink eyeglasses. She'd popped out of thin air—like magic.

"Whoa!" Jak yelped, almost falling out of his chair. His heart nearly jumped out of his chest. "Where did you come from?"

The girl shrugged. "I was just practicing my invisibility, what else?"

"Right, right." Jak struggled to contain his surprise. "Of course."

She adjusted her oversize glasses as she eyed him suspiciously. "What are you doing in my seat?"

Jak gulped and scooted one chair over. "Oops."

"Now, Sophie," Mrs. King gently chided her. "Practice makes perfect, but you know you're not supposed to sneak around the house while you're invisible. We've talked about this."

"Sorry, Mom," Sophie said, although she didn't really sound like it. She sat down next to Jak. "Honestly, sometimes I just forget I'm invisible." She lowered her voice. "Sort of."

Now that he could actually see her, Jak noticed that Sophie looked a lot like his own sister, Sadie. Both were a couple of years younger than Jak, and both barely came up to his shoulder in height. Sophie and Sadie could have been identical twins, aside from the fact that Jak's sister didn't have glasses and couldn't turn invisible at will. Nobody in Jak's family had any magic.

"Is that lasagna I smell?" Mr. King joined them in the kitchen. He sat down across from the kids.

"As usual, you're just in time," Mrs. King said. "My book club is meeting tonight at seven." She glanced at the old-fashioned clock on the kitchen wall, which had just ticked past six thirty. "Would you mind rolling back the clock long enough for us to have a nice, relaxing family dinner? I'd rather not have to rush."

"No problem." Mr. King fiddled with his wristwatch—an antique bronze timepiece. Mr. King turned the dial on the watch, and Jak felt a strange sensation—like static electricity—wash over him. His skin tingled and his eyes bulged as the hands of the clock started *moving backward*. Amazed, he looked at the digital clock above the stove and saw the minutes ticking backward there, too, until they were more than thirty minutes in the past.

For real?

"There." Mr. King stopped turning the dial, and the tingling sensation went away. "That should give you enough time to enjoy a leisurely meal and still make it to your book club with time to spare."

"Thanks, honey." Mrs. King scooped the lasagna onto a serving plate and placed it in the center of the table, where everyone could get at it. "We wouldn't want to wolf down our food. That would be bad for our digestion."

Jak could barely conceal his excitement. His whole family had magic here! He helped himself to a big slice of lasagna but hesitated before taking a bite. Sure, it smelled delicious, but he couldn't help remembering the one time his dad had tried to make lasagna. It was so burned that it was hard to swallow—except the parts that weren't cooked enough.

Jak cautiously took a bite . . . of the best lasagna he had ever tasted. It was warm and tasty and oh so filling. He scarfed down his portion and went back for seconds. As it turned out, traveling through a magic mirror from one world to another really worked up an appetite.

Great home cooking and *magic,* he thought. *I could get used to this. . . .*

"So did the Drama Club like that old mirror we donated to them?" Mr. Kong asked Zach.

It was dinnertime at the Kongs' house in Reverse World. Unable to put it off any longer, Zach had gone "home" after school to meet the Kongs, the Reverse World copies of his family. Just like at school, everything was the same—but different. Zach sat at the kitchen table, and here *Mr.* Kong fixed dinner. The setting felt so familiar that it was easy to forget that he wasn't back in his own kitchen.

"I guess so," Zach replied. He left out the part where he'd cracked the mirror trying to dive through it—and the bad luck that seemed to have brought him. "Ms. Flake said it looked 'imposing' on the stage."

"Don't you mean Ms. Fluke?" Jak's dad asked as he puttered around the kitchen. "Anyway, I'm glad that dusty old thing found a good home."

Zach realized that the Kongs had donated the mirror to the school to get rid of it, just like his own mom wanted to clean out the attic. This being Reverse World, however, the mirror had been in the basement, not the attic.

That makes sense, Zach thought, *in an upside-down kind of way.*

"Still don't know why you go to that school in the first place," Sadie said. Jak's little sister sat beside Zach at the table. She was a dead ringer for Sophie, except that her hair was in a ponytail and she didn't have magic pink glasses. "You should get homeschooled like me."

Zach shrugged. "Maybe I like going to school."

"But what's the point of going to a magic school when you don't have any magic? Homeschooling makes more sense for kids like us."

Zach felt an odd sense of déjà vu. Back home, Sophie was homeschooled because she was magic, while Zach went to public school because his parents thought he'd been skipped over. But here in Reverse World, Sadie was being homeschooled because she *wasn't* magic, and Jak was going to magic school despite having no magic? It was enough to make his head spin.

"School is where my friends are," he insisted.

Or at least that was true back home. He wondered if it

was the same for Jak. He was obviously on good terms with Baron and Trina, but it sure hadn't seemed as though Jak and Raquel were friends in Reverse World.

"Whatever," Sadie said with a shrug. She turned toward her dad. "How long are we going to wait for Mom this time? I'm starving!"

Zach knew how she felt. He'd been so busy coping with Reverse World that he hadn't eaten a thing since that one slice of cafeteria pizza at lunch. But Mrs. Kong was not back from work yet, so dinner was on hold.

Mr. Kong glanced at the kitchen clock. He winced slightly at the time. "Let's just give your mom a few more minutes . . . as usual."

Sadie groaned. "I knew I should have eaten a bigger lunch."

Just as Zach was thinking about raiding the refrigerator for a predinner snack, the front door of the house slammed open. Mrs. Kong rushed into the kitchen, breathless and flustered. "Sorry to keep you waiting! I completely lost track of time."

"That's fine, dear," Mr. Kong said to his wife. "We're

all here now. That's what matters."

He opened the oven door, releasing a thick cloud of black smoke. He fanned the smoke away and, using oven mitts, pulled a big pan of lasagna out of the oven. Sighing, Sophie hopped off her seat and cracked open a window to air the room out. Her weary expression gave Zach the impression that Dad had done this many times before.

The smoke made Zach's eyes water. It also made him worry about dinner. Mr. Kong had obviously overcooked it, and without a magic watch to turn back time, it seemed like dinner would be very crunchy tonight.

"Brace yourself," Sadie whispered to Zach as she sat back down beside him. "We don't want to hurt Dad's feelings."

"Here you go, Jak! Just scrape off the black, burned stuff."

Mr. Kong plopped a big slice of lasagna onto Zach's plate. It was charred around the edges, but also some-how goopy enough to run over the edge of the plate. Zach eyed it apprehensively, but he *was* famished, so he scooped a forkful into his mouth.

Mr. Kong's lasagna made the pizza at the school cafeteria seem like a gourmet meal by comparison. The noodles were crunchy, the beef was burned, and the cheese had melted into a cold, curdled, soggy soup that made Zach gag.

"Yum!" he said to spare Mr. Kong's feelings. He forced the first bite down. "Tastes . . . great!"

"Thanks, Jak," he replied. "I know it's your favorite!"

Zach found that hard to believe, even in Reverse World. Either Jak had a cast-iron stomach and taste buds of steel or he was a very good liar.

Probably that last one, he thought.

Sadie gave a sympathetic look at Zach as he dug into the so-called lasagna. He found himself wishing that the Kongs had a dog to feed his dinner to, but then eating this might not even be fair to a dog. Zach reached for the salt and started to sprinkle some on in the hopes of making the lasagna slightly less inedible. But instead, the shaker's lid came off, and an avalanche of salt poured all over his plate.

More bad luck?

"Oops!" Zach said. "I think I ruined it."

"Don't worry, son," Mr. Kong said. "There's plenty more still warming in the oven."

Zach forced a smile.

This is about all I can take, he thought. *I have to get back to my own world.*

But how?

CHAPTER 7

OUR WORLD

Jak felt like a kid in a candy store. The attic, which he was exploring after dinner, was packed with possibly magical objects he couldn't wait to experiment with.

The birdcage? The waffle iron? The saxophone? The mousetrap?

Maybe not that last one, he decided. Best to be cautious. Magic could be tricky. From going to magic school as long as he had, he knew that it could take kids weeks or months or even years to fully master their magic objects. And here Jak didn't even know what any of these objects could do.

Looking around, he didn't spot anything obviously magical like a wand or a crystal ball, but then he noticed a dusty glass jar sitting on a shelf next to a metal watering can. The word *Sweets* was written on the side of the jar in flowing cursive type.

"Hmm," Jak murmured.

A magic candy jar struck him as harmless enough, not to mention tempting. His sweet tooth drew him over to the shelf, where he picked up the jar and shook it gently. To his disappointment, it sounded empty, but he pried open the lid and peeked inside anyway. All he found was one lonely gumball resting at the bottom of it. Jak frowned. Talk about a letdown!

"Come on," he grumbled. "Is that the best you can do?"

His fingers tingled where they touched the jar. Surprised, Jak dropped the jar onto the floor—and a flood of candy spilled out.

His eyes bulged at the sheer quantity and variety of the sweets: chocolate bars, jelly beans, licorice sticks, bubble gum, candy corn, peppermints, peanut brittle, caramels, butterscotch, marshmallows, cinnamon bites, lemon drops, Tic Tacs, and—his favorite—gummy squids!

Jak mashed a handful of candy into his mouth—and then he picked up the jar to inspect it. When he turned it over, a river of candy poured out without stopping. All kinds of goodies spilled out onto the attic floor.

It was a bottomless candy jar!

Jak grinned as he righted the jar, and the goodies stopped multiplying. This world just kept getting better and better. Sitting down on the floor, he celebrated by gorging on chocolates and gummies. But pretty soon Jak was starting to feel a bit . . . overstuffed. His insides rumbled and he let out an enormous burp—which exited his lips as a huge pink bubble that popped loudly in front of his face.

Oops! Jak thought. *I think I may have overdone it on the candy.*

Another burp, even bigger than the first, produced a huge rainbow-colored bubble that exploded in midair.

Filmy shreds of bubble fell like confetti onto the floor before evaporating.

Uh-oh, Jak thought, *that's not normal.*

He felt another big, magical burp coming on. . . .

REVERSE WORLD

Zach snuck up to the attic after dinner on the off chance that maybe there was another magic mirror up there—but he quickly realized that had just been wishful thinking. The attic was a craft room, complete with a sewing machine, scrapbooking supplies, and even a working loom. Zach hoped Mr. Kong was better at arts and crafts than he was at cooking. His stomach was still upset from trying to digest that bad lasagna. He was actually thinking that he might be sick when a high-pitched voice behind him said, "Who are you and what have you done with my big brother?"

Sadie. She'd tiptoed up into the attic to confront Zach, since apparently you couldn't get away from nosy little sisters even when they *weren't* invisible.

"What are you talking about?" Zach asked, as if he didn't know. "It's me, Jak, your brother."

"Not a chance," she said with certainty. She plopped down on a stool next to the loom. "For one thing, Jak is left-handed, but you used your right hand at dinner. Plus, you have obviously never faced Dad's lasagna before." She tossed him a roll of cherry-mint antacids. "Take these. You're going to need them."

Zach kicked himself for not thinking about the right-handed thing. He should have guessed that would be reversed here. He popped a pink antacid tablet into his mouth and immediately felt his stomach settle.

"So . . . who are you really?"

"Um, er, well, that is . . ." Zach stalled. He considered lying, but Sadie obviously had his number, and, if she was anything like Sophie, she wasn't going to back down until she found out what was going on. Besides, to be honest, he really needed somebody to talk to about all this craziness. "Okay, but you can't tell anybody what I'm about to tell you."

"Deal," Sadie said, "provided you're not a man-eating shape-shifter from outer space."

"Is that actually a possibility?" Zach asked nervously.

There was a lot he didn't know about Reverse World.

"Of course not," she said. "*Sheesh.* Now, spill it before I fall asleep waiting."

He took a deep breath. "Well, for starters, my name is Zach . . . and the truth is, I'm not from this world."

Sadie listened intently, only interrupting him every couple of minutes or so, as Zach explained what he'd figured out about the magic mirrors.

"Well, you can't tell anyone about the mirror here," Sadie said. "If any grown-ups find out that mirror is really magic, they'll lock it somewhere supersafe and super-secure to prevent anybody else from another world from entering ours and causing chaos."

Zach gulped. "But they'd let me go home first, right?"

"Doubt it," Sadie said, shaking her head. "They're not going to let you go back to your world. They'd think it's too dangerous. Some magicians from another world caused some serious problems here many years ago, and since then traveling through mirrors is strictly off-limits."

Zach remembered Trina saying something similar

before. "But I have to get back where I belong!"

"Then you're going to have to be sneaky about it." She paused to think it over, toying with the loom. "So you actually have magic where you come from?"

"Yep," Zach confirmed. "Our whole family does."

"That's zee-zee."

"What?" Zach asked.

"Zee-zee? It's slang—short for *crazy*," she explained.

"Ha!" Zach laughed. "In our world, kids say 'cray-cray.' Means the same thing."

"Weird," Sadie said.

"Yep—deeply weird," Zach said. He picked up a ball of yarn that was sitting on a table and tossed it gently like a baseball. "Back home, I can activate most any magical object, but here I don't seem to have any magic. And I'm assuming that Jak is in my world now and has magic. It's the only thing that makes any sense."

"Jak with magic?" Sadie said, frowning. "That could mean trouble for everybody."

Zach didn't like the sound of that. "How come?"

"Look," Sadie said, "Jak's not bad as annoying big brothers go, but he's always resented the fact that our family doesn't have magic like everybody else. He's kinda touchy about it." She shrugged to indicate that she was perfectly chill with the situation. "But if Jak has stumbled into a world where he has magic and most people don't, he's going to be like a pyromaniac in a fireworks factory. . . . He might never want to come home."

Zach's heart sank. As far as he knew, he needed Jak to use his magic to activate the magic mirror from the other side. But now that Jak had magic, would he ever want to trade places again?

CHAPTER 8

OUR WORLD

Jak's stomach was rumbling like a Candy Land volcano. He groaned and clutched his belly as he headed downstairs from the attic, leaving its treasure trove of magical objects behind for the moment. He just wanted to lie down and recover from gorging on all those sweets. He probably should have guessed that a magical candy jar would lead to magical indigestion.

Sophie met him at the bottom of the stairs. She peered at him through her hot-pink glasses. Her arms were crossed on her chest.

"There you are," she said. "We need to talk."

Jak scowled. He didn't need this. "Not right now—"

His words were cut off as he burped an enormous brownish-yellow bubble. When it popped, it released a cloud of butterscotch-scented vapor.

"Whoa. That's new." Sophie's eyes bulged behind her glasses. "You're burping sweets now?"

"So what if I am?" he challenged her, and then moaned.

Sophie nodded. "See, the real Zach wouldn't talk to me like that. That's just one more reason I know you're not who you say you are."

Jak refused to be called out by a nine-year-old. "You don't know what you're talking about—"

A voice from below interrupted their face-off. "Zach, Sophie, can you come here?" Mrs. King called from the ground floor of the house. "Your dad and I could use your help."

Jak gulped. Zach's pest of a sister was one thing, but he didn't want to burp candy in front of Zach's parents. If they figured out that he wasn't really Zach, they were sure to send him back to his world. He wasn't ready to relinquish his magic yet; he was just getting started. He doubled over as his stomach rumbled, and when he straightened up, he looked to Sophie for advice.

But she was gone. Vanished into thin air.

"Great," he muttered. "Thanks a lot."

"Zach?" Mrs. King called again. "Did you hear me? Come down now, please."

"Coming!" he shouted back, unable to see any way out of it. "Be right there!"

Hoping that his upset stomach wouldn't give him away, Jak hurried downstairs. He found Mr. and Mrs. King in the living room, where they were staring at the walls with thoughtful expressions. *This is one weird world,* Jak thought.

Mrs. King turned toward him as he entered. "Where's Sophie?" she asked.

"She vanished," Jak said. "What do you need?"

"We're decorating," she said. "But your dad and I can't decide what color the walls should be. What do you think?"

Jak was thinking he wanted to be somewhere else. He grimaced as the surging candy storm in his stomach started building up again. . . .

Speechless, Zach's parents gaped at Jak—and at the heap of candy corn now littering the carpet. Jak pulled his hoodie over his face to hide his embarrassment as Mr. King finally found his voice.

"Zach?" he said. "What just happened?"

"Er, I can explain," Jak said, stalling. His stomach felt better, but his mind had gone blank. "The thing is, you see, is that, well, it's like this. . . ."

His voice trailed off as a workable excuse eluded him.

"Gotcha!" Sophie exclaimed, appearing out of nowhere behind Jak. She laughed as she waved a brown paper bag in the air. Loose candy rattled inside the bag. "You should have seen your faces!"

Mrs. King looked at her daughter in surprise. "Sophie? You were responsible for this . . . spectacle?"

"Naturally!" She demonstrated by blowing into the bag, then squeezing it so that a few more pieces of candy flew out. "I couldn't resist!"

Jak sighed in relief. He wasn't sure why Sophie was covering for him, but he wasn't going to look a gift horse in the mouth.

"Good one, sis!" he said, playing along. He faked a big grin. "We really got them!"

"Just some leftover Halloween treats," Sophie said with a shrug. "They were old and stale anyway."

Mr. and Mrs. King still looked a bit perplexed, but not as much as before.

"That was quite a practical joke," Mr. King observed.

"Somebody better clean up this mess," Mrs. King added. "Pronto."

"Absolutely!" Jak said. He moved quickly to start cleaning. "Right, sis?"

"Yep!" Sophie glanced at the green wall. "So, what's the verdict: green or blue?"

"Blue, I think," Mrs. King said, changing it back to blue. "Or maybe the green? I can't decide. . . ."

Jak had to hand it to Sophie. She knew how to change the subject and distract her parents from looking too closely at things. He wondered if she did the same for the real Zach.

Probably, he guessed.

As Mr. and Mrs. King went back to waffling over the

room's makeover, Sophie whispered to Jak: "You owe me—and I want answers."

Sophie wore rubber kitchen gloves as she swept up all the candy corn that Jak had spewed. She held the brown paper bag away from her and made a face before dropping it in the trash. "I know where that's been."

Afterward, she and Jak crept upstairs to Zach's room, where they could talk in secret.

"Thanks for covering for me," he said to Sophie after closing the door.

She sat down at Zach's desk. "I didn't do it for you. My folks don't know that Zach is magic. If they knew, they'd make him drop out of school and get homeschooled like me and my cousins. And more important, the rest of the world doesn't know our family is magic." She shook her finger at Jak. "Don't you mess that up, Fake Zach!"

"Jak," he said. "Why would you hide being magic? It's like the greatest thing ever!"

Now that he had expelled all that candy and he no longer felt like an overstuffed piñata, his confidence came back. Despite the side effects, he had still managed to activate the magic jar—which he could never have done back in his world. He had magic here, which was just about the most awesome thing that had ever happened to him.

"You said it yourself," he gloated. "You can't reveal that Zach is magic, so you can't tell anybody that Zach and I traded places."

Sophie gave him a dirty look but couldn't deny it. "Traded places from where? Where is my brother?"

"That's for me to know and you to find out," he said. He wasn't about to tell her all about the magic mirror in the attic, just in case she found a way to use it against him. "If you ever do find out, that is."

"I know one thing," she said. "You don't belong here."

"Says you," he said. "I hate to break it to you, but I like it here. For the first time in my life, I'm magic. I'm not going anywhere anytime soon, fake sister."

"But what about your friends and family?" Sophie asked. "Don't you want to see them again?"

"Maybe eventually, someday," Jak said. "But you don't know what it was like back there. Even my best friends felt sorry for me because I didn't have magic. If I have to give them up to be magic . . . well, that's a price I'm willing to pay for now."

Sophie looked at him scornfully. "Giving up friendships for magic? Sounds like a bad trade to me—not to mention a selfish one."

"Easy for you to say," Jak said, feeling a twinge of guilt. "You've always been magic. I don't care what you think—I'm not throwing this chance away. So you might as well get used to the idea that I'm your new brother."

"I know Zach King—and you're no Zach King," she scoffed. "He'll be back—and when he does, you'll be sorry if you don't behave."

Jak didn't like the sound of that. "What makes you think that's going to happen anytime soon?"

"Zach once flushed a giant alligator down a toilet. He stopped a stampede of wild horses. You think you're going to stop him from finding a way to get back home?"

Jak blinked. "He did what?"

"You better believe it, *Jak*. My brother may get himself into trouble all the time, but he also always finds a way to get out of it. One way or another, I promise you this—

Zach's going to come back and set things straight. You can count on it."

"That's it!" Jak said, losing his temper, but Sophie darted away and went invisible. He swept his hands through the air, but he couldn't find her. "No fair!" he whined.

The bedroom door swung open as if blown by a wind and then slammed shut and locked.

"Don't get comfortable, faker," Sophie yelled from the hallway. "My brother's coming back—and if you mess up his room, he's going to be mad."

Jak scowled and tried to chase after her, but by the time he got the door open, he had no idea where she'd gone. Her being invisible was going to be a problem. But he'd deal with that later. Right now, he was more worried that Sophie might be right and Zach *could* find a way to return. Zach might now have magic in the Reverse World—but everyone else there did too. Jak had waited his whole life to be magical—and he finally was. Nobody was going to take this away from him.

I need to get rid of that magic mirror, he realized, *for good.*

CHAPTER 9

REVERSE WORLD

"Excuse me, do you have any books on magic mirrors?"

The first chance he had, Zach went to the school library to see if he could find some way to reopen the mirror. This was the Horace Greeley *Magic* School, after all, so maybe the library could point him in the right direction. Thousands of books on magic filled the shelves—surely one of those books held a clue to help him get back home.

"Over there in the Unnatural Sciences section," the

school librarian said from behind the help desk. No surprise, she looked and sounded a lot like Mrs. Lewis, the librarian at Zach's real school. "Between the books on scrying and illusion casting."

She pointed a yellow highlighter toward the southwest bookcases. Zach's eyes widened as a glowing yellow line appeared beneath the shelf in question. In Reverse World even the school librarian had a magic object. Zach acted as though this was perfectly normal.

"Thanks," he said.

He was getting better at hiding his surprise, but that just reminded him that he had already been stuck here too long. It hadn't even been twenty-four hours, and he already missed his family and his friends. Heck, he even missed Tricia and Mr. Riggs. He never thought he'd say that.

Meanwhile, bad luck from the broken mirror continued to plague him. Already today, he'd had a bird poop on his shoulder and been splashed by a passing car on his way to school. He couldn't take much more of this—let alone another seven years of it!

The highlighted bookshelf called out to him. Hoping

one of the books there held a solution to his problems, Zach crossed the library, which was pretty deserted, with only a handful of students present. Zach spotted Raquel over at a table in a corner, sitting by herself as usual. She had a book open in front of her as she took notes for an assignment.

Making eye contact, they nodded awkwardly at each other. They hadn't spoken since he had freaked her out yesterday and she had accidentally blasted him down the hallway. She looked uncomfortable seeing him again.

He couldn't blame her.

The glowing yellow line was fading away by the time he reached the highlighted shelf. His heart sank as he discovered an entire shelf of books on magic mirrors, reflections, shadows, and doubles. He hadn't expected quite so many books on the subject. He had no idea where to start. The magic mirror in the attic in his real home was destined for the garbage dump on Saturday. There had to be a *Magic Mirrors for Dummies* here or something.

Scanning the shelf, he zeroed in on the slimmest volume. It was so short that he almost missed it at first glance. He squinted to make out the title on the book's spine:

MIRROR MAGIC

He took the book from the shelf. It was dusty, as though it hadn't been checked out in a long time. The pages were stuck together and he had to tug gently on the covers to pull them apart. When he did, a thin paper leaflet tumbled out of the book and fluttered to the floor in front of Zach. Bending to picking it up, he was shocked to see a drawing on the cover of the pamphlet that looked just like the antique mirror that had transported him to Reverse World.

An instruction manual?

Excited, Zach opened the leaflet to read what was written inside, but the words and sentences didn't even look like English. Somebody had scribbled something in red ink at the bottom of the page, but it was just as unreadable as the printed text. Zach couldn't make head or tail of it. At first he thought the whole thing was written in a foreign language he didn't recognize, but then he realized what he was looking at. He smacked his forehead for not figuring it out right away. The text was printed *in reverse*—like in a mirror.

Which meant you needed a mirror to read it.

Clutching the leaflet, Zach dashed out of the library, earning him a disapproving look from the librarian as he rushed past her.

"Sssh! This is not a racetrack, young man!"

"Sorry!" Zach said without slowing down. Exiting the library, he sprinted to the theater, where, to his relief, he saw that the magic mirror was still on the stage. Ms. Fluke was there, too, along with some of the Drama Club, who were rehearsing the play. The drama teacher was dressed as the Wicked Queen. Zach guessed that she was playing that part in *Snow White* for some reason. She turned toward Zach as he raced onto the stage.

"Oh, hi, Jak," she addressed him. She was wearing a long, black cape and a fake golden crown. Her polished wooden wand was about the length of a ruler. "Can I help you?"

He hadn't expected to find the stage occupied, so he

had to improvise. "Um, I just wanted to see how that old mirror is working out."

"Oh, it's just perfect," she said. "Please thank your parents again for me. That was very generous of them to donate it to our production." She glanced over at the cracked mirror. "Although I'm afraid it got a little . . . damaged . . . somehow."

Zach acted like this was news to him. "That's too bad. But . . . you're still keeping it, right?" he asked. "You're not going to throw it away?"

"Actually, I've come up with a wonderful idea," she said proudly. "Turns out our original Wicked Queen just came down with the flu, so I'm having to take over the part at the last minute, and I've added a whole new bit where the Magic Mirror tells the Wicked Queen that Snow White is the fairest of all one too many times, so the queen loses her temper and blasts the mirror with my very own magic wand, causing it to vanish in a big puff of smoke. Poof!"

She waved her magic wand, which was apparently the real thing.

Zach gulped. "Vanish—for good?"

"Might as well, since it's broken anyway," she explained. "But it will make a nice dramatic moment Saturday night, don't you think? It should get a great response from the audience!"

"Oh, cool, yeah," Zach mumbled, tugging nervously at his collar. "That sounds . . . awesome."

Talk about bad luck, he thought. Now time was seriously running out. If they made that mirror vanish before he could figure out a way to get back home, Zach would be stuck here forever.

He clutched the leaflet he'd found in the library.

Please let this tell me how to reopen the mirror, he thought, *or I'm in big trouble.*

Desperate to find out what the pamphlet said, he waited impatiently until Ms. Fluke and the Drama Club took a break before heading over to the mirror. When nobody was looking, Zach held the leaflet up to the mirror, which reversed the backward words so he could finally read them:

Mirrors—especially magic mirrors—allow you to take a good look at yourself. But you need to look beyond the mirror as well. A person who sees only themselves is not seeing what truly matters. Pride and vanity are a magician's worst enemy. When you look in the mirror, remember that you are also looking at all the people who are standing behind you who helped you get where you are, even when you cannot see them.

Zach's gaze moved on to the message scribbled in ink at the bottom of the page. What had looked like an illegible scrawl before could be read easily now:

Short version: Even the greatest magician in the world needs their friends.—Lionel King.

Zach couldn't believe his eyes. He read the signature over again just to confirm that it really said *King* and not *Kong.* Lionel King was his real great-grandfather! But what was a message from him doing in Reverse World?

Maybe he also went through the mirror, Zach thought. *It would make sense. Lionel was well-known as one of the most powerful magicians in his family.* Zach wondered if Great-Grandpa Lionel had also left a leaflet hidden in his library at Horace Greeley Middle School, just in case. *That's what I'd do.*

"Thanks for thinking ahead, Great-Grandpa."

Once he got over his excitement, however, Zach realized that the hidden message didn't really offer a solution to his problem. He had been hoping for some sort of instructions or magical incantation that would help him reactivate the mirror so he could go home, but all he'd found was a lesson about friendship, which was important, of course, but which wasn't going to get him back where he belonged.

Or was it?

Even the greatest magician in the world needs their friends, Zach read again, thinking it over. Boy, did he appreciate now just how true that was. He wouldn't be in this fix if he had relied on his friends instead of his magic. He had told Aaron and Rachel that he didn't need their help. He had told them he could handle anything on his own, that all he needed was magic!

If only I hadn't been too proud to ask for help!

He had learned that lesson the hard way, but what

good could that do him now? All his real friends were on the other side of the mirror. He didn't have any real friends in Reverse World, but then it occurred to him: maybe reversed friends could be made real friends if he tried?

I can't do this on my own, he realized. *Time to make some new friends.*

CHAPTER 10

OUR WORLD

The skateboard was awesome. It had a golden lightning bolt printed on the bottom. Dusted off, it looked as good as new. Jak had rescued it from the attic and was dying to find out what kind of magic it held.

School had let out early that day, and Zach's family had gone to the grocery store to do some shopping, so Jak had the place to himself. Garbage pickup wasn't until tomorrow, so he couldn't dispose of the magic mirror yet, which meant he had time to play with his new magic some more. He'd brought the skateboard down to the driveway in front of the Kings' house, which was an ordinary-looking, white-and-red farmhouse at the end of a long private road. Trees and shrubs helped to shield the home from prying eyes—not that Jak was terribly worried about that. Where he came from, nobody tried to hide their magic.

The skateboard rested on the road in front of him. Despite his curiosity, Jak couldn't help remembering his mishaps with the magic wardrobe and candy jar. He was working up his nerve to try out the skateboard when Aaron and Rachel dropped by unexpectedly.

"Yo, dude," Aaron called to him. "What's up?"

Jak assumed that Aaron must be this world's version of Baron, although it was weird to see him cradling a plump gray cat, of all things. The real Baron was a dog person in more ways than one. He didn't cuddle cats. He chased them. The cat regarded Jak suspiciously.

"You feeling better?" Rachel asked. "You were acting so weird earlier."

"What are you two doing here?" Jak asked. He didn't have time for interruptions.

"You weren't answering our texts, dude," Aaron said, "so we wanted to make sure you were okay."

"Sorry," Jak said gruffly. "I've been busy."

"Chatting with Tricia?" Rachel asked.

Jak couldn't tell if she was teasing him or not. Before he could reply, Aaron's cat hissed at him. The cat's hackles rose angrily as Aaron approached Jak. Yellow eyes glared at Jak as though the cat somehow knew he was an imposter.

"Whoa! What's the matter, Michael?" Aaron asked the upset animal, who was squirming and twisting in his arms. "It's just Zach!"

Michael swiped at Jak with his claws. Jak had to jump backward to avoid getting scratched.

"Hey!" Jak said. "Why'd you bring that crazy cat anyway?"

"Dude!" Aaron protested. He clutched the feline to his chest as he backed away from Jak to give them more space. "Don't talk about Michael like that. You'll hurt his feelings!"

"What's wrong with you, Zach?" Rachel asked. "You're not acting like yourself!"

You have no idea, Jak thought. "I'm fine. Never better."

"Could have fooled me," Rachel said.

Jak figured it was time to change the subject. The perfect distraction occurred to him. "Hey, Aaron! You up for shooting some awesome video?"

"Always!" Aaron answered. He handed off Michael to Rachel as he took out his phone. "Now you're talking. What do you have in mind?"

Jak smirked. The more he thought about it, the more he liked the idea of Aaron filming him trying out the skateboard. He wanted to show off his new magic for the whole world to see.

"Get your camera ready," he said. "And check this out."

Grinning, he hopped onto the skateboard and kicked off.

A scaly orange fish flopped around on top of Jak's head, before bouncing back into the koi pond. The lightning-fast skateboard had finally come to rest, floating upside down in the pond. Steam rose from its overheated wheels.

"Zach!" Rachel shouted as she and Aaron ran into the backyard to see how he was. Michael stayed back, not wanting to get wet. "Are you all right?"

"I'm fine," he said, embarrassed and annoyed by his splashdown into the pond. He recovered the skateboard and clambered out of the pond, dripping onto the patio. He was soaking wet and not in a good mood. Soggy clothes hung on his body as he scowled at Aaron. "Please tell me you got that on video at least."

"Only a split second," Aaron confessed. "You took off so fast that I couldn't keep up." He shrugged apologetically. "On the bright side, since you were going so fast, nobody's going to recognize you. You were just a blur to them."

That was not what Jak wanted to hear.

"Great," he grumbled.

"You're lucky you were moving too fast to be ID'd," Rachel said. "What were you thinking, Zach? You need to be less reckless with your magic."

Jak was in no mood to be scolded. "What do you know about it? You don't even have magic here! Neither of you do!"

"What do you mean, 'here'?" Rachel shook her head in confusion. "Seriously, Zach, it's like I don't even know who you are anymore!"

CHAPTER 11

REVERSE WORLD

Later that day, Zach found Raquel in the cafeteria, sitting by herself. She looked up without closing her book as he approached her. Baron and his fan club were at their usual table nearby, chattering away. Trina was there too, smiling warmly at everyone. Zach needed to talk to them, too, but he had to convince Raquel first. His plan depended on it.

He sat down across from her, only to have a chair leg give out beneath him. He grabbed onto the table to keep from falling, but that tilted the table, causing Raquel's juice bottle to tip over. Grape drink spilled across the table.

"Sorry, sorry!" Zach said. "Please don't blast me again! I'm just having a run of bad luck!"

"It's okay," Raquel said, dabbing up the mess with some paper napkins. "It was just an accident."

Seeing no other option, Zach nervously took another chair. *Remind me never to break a magic mirror again,* he thought. "Sorry to bother you, but I have a question to ask you."

"Go for it."

"So," Zach whispered, "how exactly does your magic work?"

"Let me ask you a question," she said, crossing her arms. "Why do you care?"

"I really need your help." He took a deep breath before going for broke. "It all started with a magic mirror in my parents' attic. . . ."

He told her the whole story, leaving nothing out, about how he wasn't really Jak and where he came from and how he needed to get back to where he belonged before anything happened to the mirrors in both worlds. He couldn't afford to waste time trying to tiptoe around the truth or hide the fact that magic mirrors were involved. He had to come clean with Raquel and hope she believed him.

"I know it sounds ridiculous," he said, "but—"

"No, it makes perfect sense," she said. "That explains the bad luck, too."

Zach blinked in surprise. "It does?"

"Of course." She fished another book from her backpack and placed it on the table. Zach wasn't sure, but he thought it was the same book she'd been studying in the library earlier. "There's been plenty written about parallel worlds and opposite lands—and about how broken magic mirrors can warp the laws of chance. That's mostly advanced high school material—like trigonometry or French—but I read *way* above my grade level. Not to brag or anything."

Zach peeked at the book, which was filled with

complicated charts and equations and mystical symbols. Just trying to read it made his head spin, so he took Raquel's word for it that there were some kinds of established magical theories behind what had happened to him. He was worried about a more immediate issue.

"So you believe me?"

"No reason not to," she answered. "Magic mirrors wouldn't be banned if they weren't real. Except . . . you and I are best friends where you come from?" She shook her head in disbelief. "Freaky."

Zach didn't take that personally. He had no idea what Jak was really like.

"It's true, cross my heart. We're all friends—you, me, and Aaron."

She gave him a puzzled look. "Aaron?"

"Baron for you." He glanced over at the other table and saw that Baron had turned back into a dog again. He was running around the table, barking and wagging his tail, much to the amusement of the other kids. His magic dog whistle dangled on a chain around his neck. Trina threw him a piece of cheese and clapped as Baron caught it in midair.

Michael would not approve, Zach thought.

"Hang on," Raquel said. "I'm friends with the most popular boy in school?"

"Er, not exactly," Zach said. "But my Aaron always has my back, and so do you . . . I mean, Rachel. The other you."

Looking across the table, Zach still couldn't believe how much Raquel looked like Rachel. He hoped that the resemblance was more than skin deep and that he could count on Raquel as well.

"Anyway," he said, "what I was wondering was how your magic actually works."

"The truth is, I don't know exactly." She sighed. "I'm like a walking battery of raw magical energy. It just builds up inside me. I don't have a magic object of my own to focus it on, and it just spills over sometimes . . . in weird and unpredictable ways." She shrugged. "Or at least that's what the school's magic counselor thinks."

That sounds a lot like my magic back home, Zach thought. He started feeling hopeful again. "But if you've got raw magic to burn, does that mean that

you can activate *any* magic object? Like maybe you can use your magic to jump-start the mirror to get me home?"

Raquel's face went pale. She gulped and backed away from Zach, scooting her chair away from the table. The very idea seemed to spook her.

"No way," she said. "I'm sorry. I want to help, but you don't know what you're asking. My magic is too strong—even for me. You saw what happened when you spooked me the other day. It's safer for everyone if I just keep it to myself."

"But I'm running out of time. If I don't get home before tomorrow night, I'm going to be stuck here forever. You're my only chance!"

"I can't!" She shook her head. "I wish I could help . . . but I just can't."

"Yes, you can," Zach told her. "Where I come from, you're the bravest girl I know."

"That's great, but that's not the real me! She's just my reflection!"

Zach remembered his great-grandpa's note. "Mirrors let you see yourself. If you look hard enough, you can be as brave as you want to be. I know it's there because I've seen it with my own eyes, back in my world."

Rachel wavered, uncertain.

"You really think that I can do it?" she asked Zach.

"I know it," Zach said.

"Okay then," she said, nodding. "I'll do my best."

"Thank you—seriously, thank you." Zach felt both relieved and grateful. Getting Raquel's help was crucial to his plan. "But to pull this off, we're going to need some backup."

"From who?" Raquel asked.

Zach grinned as he turned toward Baron's table, where the dog had turned back into a boy again. He waved at Baron and Trina.

"From some new friends, of course."

"We're going to need costumes," Trina said.

"Come again?" Zach replied.

It had taken a while to convince Trina and Baron that he was really Zach, not Jak, and to explain how and why he needed their help to get back where he belonged. To his relief, they proved eager to assist Zach once they realized what was at stake. Now the four of them—including Raquel—were making plans after school. For the first time in forever, Zach's luck seemed to be changing for the better. It felt good to have friends on his side again.

I should have known I could always count on them, Zach thought, *no matter what world I'm in. Their friendship has always been my real magic power—*

His eyes lit up as a sudden revelation hit him. Back home, he hadn't discovered his own magic until he'd met his friends in school. In fact, come to think of it, the very first time he'd ever done magic—he'd fallen through the glass front of the school snack machine and gotten stuck inside—was right after he'd met Aaron for the first time.

That was how it all began, he realized. *I didn't have magic until I helped a friend. True friendship was the spark that ignited my magic.* And somehow Zach knew that true friendship was also what would save him now!

"There's no way we're going to get to that magic mirror while they're getting ready for the play," Trina explained. "But if we try to blend in with the play, maybe nobody will realize what we're up to—at least, not until it's too late."

Zach saw her point. They couldn't just barge onto the stage without a reason for being there. "What kind of costumes?"

"Whatever we can scrounge up backstage," Trina said. "The main thing is to make it look like part of the play, not actual Mirror Magic."

"Works for me," Baron said, nibbling on a fresh carrot as though it was a chew toy. He fingered his magic dog whistle. "Talk about extreme. Real *Mission: Impossible* stuff."

"I suppose," Raquel said. "Just don't blame me if I come down with stage fright. I'm way out of my comfort zone here."

"We all are," Zach assured her. "Trust me."

Trina squinted at him. "Can't believe it took me this long to realize you're not the real Jak. No wonder you seemed so confused before!"

Baron sniffed him like a dog. "Yeah, you smell slightly different than our Jak, no offense."

"None taken," Zach said. "But let's go over the plan one more time, just to make sure everybody knows their part. . . ."

CHAPTER 12

OUR WORLD

Bright and early Saturday morning, Jak lugged the heavy mirror down two flights of stairs and out the front door to the sidewalk. It sucked that he couldn't just use magic to move it, but he had yet to find a magical object in the attic that could do the job. And he couldn't risk smashing the mirror himself; everyone in his world knew that breaking an actual magic mirror *really* meant seven years' bad luck. It was safer to just let the garbage workers dispose of it. One way or another, though, he wanted the mirror gone before the other Jak could find a way back to this world. The sooner the mirror was buried in a landfill, the better Jak would feel.

"What are you throwing that out for?" Sophie asked, appearing out of nowhere. She inspected the antique mirror. "It looks in good shape to me. Does Mom know you're getting rid of it?"

Jak was tempted to put a bell on Sophie so she couldn't keep sneaking up on him like this. "It's just a dusty old mirror. What do you care?"

"Why did you go to all this trouble to get rid of it?" Sophie shot back. "And nothing else?" She eyed him suspiciously; then her eyes lit up behind her magic glasses. "Hang on! A mirror, reflections . . . ? I get it now. You came to our world through that mirror!"

"Mind your own business," he said, scowling.

"It's true!" She ran over to the mirror and shouted at it. "Hello, Zach? Are you in there? Can you hear me?"

"That's enough!" Jak got between her and the mirror. Crossing his arms across his chest, he planted his feet squarely on the sidewalk. "Get lost, pest! This mirror is going straight to the dump, and there's nothing you can do about it."

A noisy rattling backed him up. He smirked as he saw the garbage truck rumbling down the private drive to the King house.

"Oh, no!" Sophie gasped at the appearance of the garbage truck. "You can't do this!"

"Wanna bet?" Jak gloated. "I'm not going back to being 'skipped.' I like having magic. Once that mirror is gone, I'm here for good. Get used to it."

"We'll see about that," Sophie said, vanishing from sight as the garbage truck pulled up to the curb. Jak watched as the garbage workers heaved the mirror into the back of the truck. He waved as it pulled away, taking

the mirror with it, but Jak didn't feel as relieved as he'd expected to. Sophie's final words left him worried.

What is she up to now?

"What's up?" Aaron asked Sophie. "What's the big emergency?"

Sophie was waiting impatiently on the sidewalk when Aaron and Rachel rode up on their bikes. She knew she couldn't get the mirror back on her own, so she had texted the only people she really trusted, given the situation—Zach's two best friends—for help.

"Is this about Zach?" Rachel skidded to a halt on her bike. "Do you know why he hasn't been himself lately?"

"Do I ever!" Sophie said. "Get a load of this. . . ."

She quickly told them what she had figured out about Jak from the magic mirror and how he'd traded places with the real Zach somehow.

"An evil twin!" Aaron slapped himself on the forehead. "Of course, it all makes sense now. No wonder 'Zach' has been acting so weird!"

Rachel nodded. "That dumb new haircut should have tipped me off!"

Michael, who was riding in a basket at the front of Aaron's bike, meowed in agreement. Sophie was glad she didn't have to waste time convincing them. They needed to move quickly.

"We can't let Fake Zach get away with this," she explained. "We need to get that mirror back from the dump before something happens to it—and we lose our Zach to some other world for keeps!"

"Then what are we waiting for?" Rachel asked. She scooted forward on her seat to make room for Sophie. "Climb aboard!"

"To the dump!" Aaron said. "ASAP!"

The sign on the gate read Municipal Waste-Management Disposal Site, but Rachel wasn't fooled. She knew a garbage dump when she saw one—and smelled it.

"Pee-yew!" Sophie said. She sat behind Rachel, holding on to the older girl as they rode up to the dump. Her nose wrinkled in disgust. "The things I have to do for my brother."

"It smells like the dumpster behind the school cafeteria on a hot summer day . . . ," Aaron chimed in, "times one thousand!"

"Never mind the smell," Rachel said, taking charge. "We've got to find that mirror."

They pulled up to the chain-link fence surrounding the dump and got off their bikes. It had been a long ride, and their legs were tired. The dump was closed for the day, so they had to climb over the fence to get in. A sign warned them to "Keep Out," but none of the kids were going to let that stop them.

They dropped onto the ground beyond the fence. Towering heaps of trash stretched out before them, waiting to be bulldozed into a long, gaping trench at the far end of the dump. Looking around, Rachel saw mounds of discarded mattresses, rubber tires, beaten-up furniture, bulging trash bags, and random garbage, but not an old-fashioned wooden mirror like the one Sophie had described to them. Rachel barely knew where to start looking.

"Spread out," she said, "and holler if you see it."

The kids, along with Michael, split up to search the

dump. Rachel scanned the tops of the looming mountains of trash, figuring that today's loads would probably be on the top of the piles. She crossed her fingers, hoping against hope that the magic mirror was still in one piece and hadn't been buried under a ton of garbage already. She wanted their old Zach back, as opposed to the obnoxious creep who had taken his place.

I should have realized that wasn't Zach, she thought. *Even on a bad day, the real Zach knows who his friends are.*

They searched the dump for hours, as the afternoon slowly turned into twilight. Rachel was on the verge of giving up when she heard Aaron call out in excitement.

"Over here! I've found it!"

Rachel ran to investigate and was joined by Sophie, who came running from another direction. They found Aaron and Michael at the base of an enormous garbage heap. Aaron bounced up and down in excitement as he pointed up at an old wooden mirror balanced precariously at the top of the mound, high above the kids' heads. It was wedged in between some bulging black garbage bags and a discarded beanbag chair.

"That's it, right?" Aaron asked. "That's the mirror!"

"Bingo!" Sophie confirmed.

Rachel peered up at the towering garbage heap. The mirror looked like it was still intact, thank goodness, but for how much longer? She noted with alarm that the deep trench of the landfill was right behind the huge trash pile. They needed to rescue the mirror before it got trashed—permanently.

"I'm on it," she said. "Wait here."

Scaling the trash heaps was even trickier and ickier than she expected. Soggy cardboard and paper towels, plastic wrappers, torn clothing, fraying rugs, rotting leftovers, coffee grounds, pizza crusts, banana peels, apple cores, kitty litter, and even more disgusting messes slipped and shifted beneath her feet, making her grateful for her sturdy cowboy boots. Her bare hands longed for work gloves, and she was feeling disgusting by the time she'd gotten to the top of the first hill—but the important thing was that she'd made it! She headed cautiously toward the mirror, not wanting to accidentally disturb the mounds and start a trash avalanche.

"Almost got it. . . ."

"Leave that mirror alone!" Jak yelled at her. The surprise made her tumble back down to the bottom of the garbage heap. "Or I'll make you regret it!"

The magic skateboard sped to the top of the largest trash pile at the dump. Jak had arrived just in time. He knew Sophie wouldn't give up that easily, and that she'd try something crazy like trying to retrieve the mirror from the dump.

Should have known Zach's loser friends would be in on it too, he thought, finding himself outnumbered. *Good thing I came prepared.*

Jak had plastic safety goggles on. He was holding a squirt gun in one hand and a folding Chinese fan in the other. He might have looked crazy, but with his magic abilities, he felt ready for anything and anybody.

"Get out of here, you faker!" Aaron shouted at him, as Michael hissed in agreement. "We're on to you now. You can't fool us anymore!"

"Big deal!" Jak skidded to a halt. "You can think what you like, but that mirror's not leaving the landfill, ever."

"Oh yeah?" Sophie challenged him. "And how are you going stop us?"

Jak smirked. "By magic!"

He pointed the squirt gun at Aaron and squeezed the trigger. A high-pressure stream of water knocked Aaron off his feet. Michael squawked and ran for cover, while Sophie pulled her usual vanishing act and disappeared from sight.

"Oh dear!" Jak said sarcastically. "Where has Sophie gone? Whatever am I going to do?"

He was just joking, of course. The magic safety goggles let him see any danger, even if it was invisible. With them on, he saw Sophie plain as day. He swung the water pistol toward her and knocked her into a pile of trash. Her glasses went flying and she turned visible again.

"Take that!" Jak gloated. "Serves you right for trying to stop me!"

"Sophie! Aaron!" Rachel shouted from the top of a gigantic mound of trash. "You leave them alone, you imposter!"

"And you mind your own business!" Jak yelled back.

He didn't want to hurt anybody, but he couldn't let them rescue that mirror. He turned the squirt gun toward Rachel, but the spray didn't quite reach her. Jak scowled but wasn't too concerned. "I'm just getting started!"

He opened the paper fan with a flick of his wrist. He fanned the air, and a ferocious wind whipped up. The wind blew Rachel backward. She actually had to grab onto the mirror to keep from being blown completely out of the landfill.

"Give it up!" Jak shouted over the roaring wind. "I've got more magic than I know what to do with!"

CHAPTER 13

REVERSE WORLD

"Mirror, mirror on the wall . . ."

Snow White was underway at the Horace Greeley Magic School theater. They'd scheduled one performance only, so the audience was jam-packed with students, faculty, and families. It was early in the story, and Ms. Fluke, playing the Wicked Queen, was hamming it up on the castle set, addressing the Magic Mirror.

". . . who is the fairest one of all?"

Zach spied on the show from an elevated catwalk

overlooking the stage. Any minute now, he knew, the drama teacher was going to use her magic wand to make the mirror really disappear, stranding Zach in Reverse World for good. If he was going to get home, he had to get back into the mirror soon.

This is it, he thought. *We're not going to get another shot at this.*

He wished they weren't calling it so close. Unfortunately, however, preparations and rehearsals for tonight's performance had pretty much kept the theater occupied nonstop. Zach had hoped they'd be lucky enough to get to the mirror before the play started, but that had just been wishful thinking. They couldn't wait any longer. It was now or never.

"I must speak the truth," the Magic Mirror replied (via a miniature speaker attached to the back of the mirror). Backstage, a kid actor was reading his lines into a microphone. "Snow White is the fairest one by far!"

"Noooo!" the Wicked Queen shrieked onstage. She raised her wand, which began to glow ominously at its tip. "Begone, you cursed mirror. . . ."

That's my cue, Zach thought. *Time to swing into action!*

He had already tied one end of a rope to another catwalk across from where he was standing, and he had "borrowed" a spare costume from the Drama Club's wardrobe supplies to blend in with the show. Without a moment to spare, he gripped the other end of the rope with both hands and swung down from the catwalk.

"Woo-hoo!"

The audience gasped as Prince Charming came swinging down onto the stage, landing in the nick of time between the Wicked Queen and the endangered mirror. He touched down on the floor and let go of the rope. His palms stung a little from the rope burn. He probably should have added some gloves to the costume.

"Halt, evildoer!" he shouted. "Surrender your wand!"

Ms. Fluke froze in confusion, uncertain what to do.

"Jak . . . I mean, Prince Charming?" She struggled to stay in character for the sake of the play. "What are you doing here?"

Zach was counting on the fact that the show must go on, no matter what, to give him and his new friends a

chance to carry out his plan right in front of everyone. He glanced at the audience. Rows of confused faces were staring at him. Jak would have a lot of explaining to do when he came back to his world, *if* he ever did.

Sorry, Jak. It can't be helped.

"Step aside, foolish prince!" Ms. Fluke ad-libbed, fighting to get her play back on track. Wand in hand, she darted up and down the stage, searching for a clean shot at the mirror. "You *really* don't belong here!"

Zach felt bad about messing up the play, but this was his last chance to get home. He couldn't let her zap the mirror with her wand. Playing defense, he kept himself between the frustrated teacher and the mirror, but he knew he couldn't keep blocking her indefinitely.

Good thing he wasn't on his own.

Zach raised his fingers to his lips and whistled sharply. A loud bark answered him as an energetic border collie bounded onto the stage. A metal whistle hung on a chain around the dog's neck. The collie barked and barked, shamelessly stealing the scene.

The audience roared in laughter, while poor Ms. Fluke looked even more flustered than before.

"Baron? Is that you?"

Who else? Zach thought. "Fetch, noble canine!"

Springing into the air, the collie snatched the wand from the startled teacher's grasp.

"Wait!" she protested. "This isn't in the script!"

CHAPTER 14

OUR WORLD

The howling wind slammed against Rachel, threatening to blow her and the mirror off the trash heap into the landfill below. The wind caught a torn old beanbag chair and tossed it down into the shadowy trench. Rachel dug her boots into the garbage and held on tightly to the magic mirror to keep it safe. Windblown bits of trash swirled around her. She swatted a grimy scrap of cloth away from her nose and shouted to Aaron and Sophie.

"Get that magic fan away from Jak!"

Easier said than done, though, with the imposter using his magic squirt gun to keep the other kids at bay. Jak swung the high-pressure stream of water back and forth between Aaron and Sophie, keeping them away. Rachel wondered how he was managing to employ so many magic objects at once. She couldn't remember Zach ever doing that.

"Let go of that mirror!" Jak yelled at her. "You know you can't hold on to it forever."

"Not a chance!" Rachel said.

"Okay!" Jak snarled. "Have it your way!"

He waved the fan, and the wind got stronger, tugging on the mirror, as Rachel held on with all her strength.

But Jak *was* trying to do too much too fast. When he wasn't paying attention, the skateboard zipped out from beneath him. He tumbled onto his butt, and then the spray from the squirt gun shot him backward into another garbage heap. A carton of rotten eggs spilled onto his head, smearing over his goggles. An empty soup can bounced off his noggin. He lost control of the wind, and he blew the spray from the water pistol back on himself. He sputtered and splashed amidst a pool of stinky, muddy, half-decayed garbage. He tried to stagger to his feet . . . and Michael darted in front of him, tripping him so that he fell face forward into the slop—again. He lost his grip on the squirt gun and paper fan.

SQUOOSH!

Rachel watched Jak flailing in the mud. He appeared to have bitten off more than he could chew. Now was their chance to get the real Zach back—and send this imposter where he belonged.

But how?

CHAPTER 15

REVERSE WORLD

Ms. Fluke chased frantically after the collie as he sprinted around the stage, carrying the stolen wand in his jaws.

"Bad dog! Come back with my wand!"

The audience was in hysterics. Zach wondered how many spectators thought this was supposed to be part of the play.

Now it was up to his other new friends.

"Prince Charming—my hero!" Trina rushed in from the wings, wearing her magic pink mitten and the spare costume meant for Snow White's understudy. "At last I've found you!"

"Trina . . . that is, Snow White?" Ms. Fluke couldn't keep up with all the sudden changes to the play. "Shouldn't you be in the forest right now, with the dwarves?"

"Not when there is injustice to be righted!" Trina said. "This is my castle too, and I'm standing up for my rights as a princess!"

She marched past the dumbfounded Wicked Queen to get to the mirror. The Scotch tape had been removed, but the silvered glass was still cracked down the middle. Zach feared that the magic mirror might not work properly in its present state, which was where Trina's healing power came in.

"Fear not, honest mirror! All will be well!"

She placed her magic mitten against the broken glass and traced the length of the crack with a wool-covered finger. Zach watched in relief as the mirror healed itself right before his eyes, the glass flowing into the crack to mend it until it was as good as new. Zach hoped that was the end of his bad luck as well.

"Good job, Snow White!" he said.

"Thank you, Prince Charming!" She stepped away from the fixed mirror. "That's what friends are for."

By now, whatever goodwill the audience had had was gone. Playgoers in the seats exchanged puzzled looks as they scratched their heads and peered at their programs. Zach couldn't blame them for being lost. This was not the *Snow White* they'd expected!

Your turn, Raquel, he thought.

He looked toward the wings, waiting for Raquel's big entrance. The audience was breathless, wondering what craziness would come next. Zach stood frozen in place for a long, scary moment, worried that Raquel had chickened out at the last minute. But then she crept nervously out onto the stage, wearing a dwarf's hat and a fake beard she had snagged backstage. The whole audience turned to look at her, and she froze in the spotlight.

"Welcome, friend!" Zach shouted to encourage her. "You arrived just in time!"

"Don't remind me," she muttered. "I mean, *yes*! It is I, a dwarf, who is absolutely supposed to be in this scene. For sure."

Ms. Fluke looked like she was about to cry. "What's happening? Which dwarf are you?"

Raquel shrugged. "The eighth one?"

The play was obviously falling apart. Zach saw Principal Ruggs creeping toward the stage, looking none too happy. Zach realized it was only a matter of minutes before the curtain came down and they were dragged off the stage to detention or worse.

"Over here!" he called to Raquel. "Hurry!"

Mr. Ruggs found a guard's plastic helmet backstage. Putting it on for the sake of the story, he stomped onto the stage and lunged for the collie, who was still running around with the stolen wand in his jaws.

"Got you!"

The principal grabbed Baron by the tail, causing the dog to yelp loudly. The wand fell out of the collie's mouth as Baron turned back into a boy, leaving Ruggs with nothing to hold. Baron dived for the fallen wand, but Ms. Fluke got to it first. She snatched it off the floor and spun toward the mirror, obviously determined to get the play back on track, no matter what. She waved the wand wildly in the air.

"Stand aside! I must banish that mirror! The script says so!"

Raquel joined Zach by the mirror. He saw his last chance at getting home slipping away again.

"Quick!" he said. "Use your magic to send me home!"

She reached for the mirror, then drew her hand back in fear.

"I don't know," she said, losing her nerve. "I don't think I can do this."

"Don't be afraid." Zach looked her squarely in the eyes. "You can do this. You're the bravest dwarf in the kingdom!"

"I guess we'll see," she said. "Get ready!"

She touched the mirror frame with her hand, and Zach felt a tingling in the air, like when his dad used his magic watch. The reflective surface of the mirror rippled like water as a giant grin broke out across Raquel's face.

"Holy smokes! I did it!"

"Because you did it for a friend," Zach realized. "That's the secret."

Glancing over his shoulder, Zach saw both Mr. Ruggs

and Ms. Fluke charging toward him. Clearly, there was no time for long goodbyes.

"Thanks!" he shouted to his reversed friends, who had come through for him just like their doubles in the real world. "Thanks, all of you!"

"Jak Kong!" the principal shouted. "I am *very* disappointed in you!"

"Go, Zach," Raquel urged him. "Now!"

She didn't need to tell him twice. Taking a deep breath, he dived headfirst into the mirror again.

CHAPTER 16

OUR WORLD

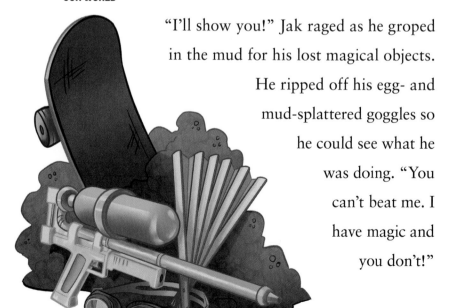

"I'll show you!" Jak raged as he groped in the mud for his lost magical objects. He ripped off his egg- and mud-splattered goggles so he could see what he was doing. "You can't beat me. I have magic and you don't!"

"Excuse me?" Sophie said.

Rachel feared Jak might be right. They could only hold him back for so long. If only Zach were here so they could deal with Jak together!

"Thanks!" Zach's voice came from the mirror. *"Thanks, all of you!"*

Rachel couldn't believe her ears. She stared in amazement as the surface of the mirror began to shimmer and ripple like water. She heard *her own voice* coming from the other side of the mirror.

"Go, Zach! Now!"

Looking down, she saw Jak stumbling to his feet at the base of the trash heap. She suddenly knew what to do.

"Welcome back, big brother," Sophie said. "About time you made it home."

Aaron checked out Zach's costume. "Dude, what's up with the cosplay outfit? There a Renaissance fair on the other side of that mirror?"

"Don't be silly," Rachel said. "He's Prince Charming." She beamed at Zach. "It looks good on you, actually."

Zach blushed.

"I'll give you all the full story later," he promised. Broken glass crackled beneath Prince Charming's boots. "Right now I'm just glad to be back and to see you all again." He glanced around, somewhat surprised by his surroundings. An overwhelming stench assaulted his nostrils. "Er, why are we in the garbage dump?"

"Long story," Rachel said. "But it all turned out well."

Zach was glad to hear it. "Jak give you any trouble?"

Sophie shrugged. "Nothing we couldn't handle."

Zach could believe it. If there was one thing he had learned from his trip through the looking glass and back, it was that good friends were stronger than any magic.

He was never taking them for granted again!

"So what happened to Jak?" Aaron asked. "Where did he go?"

Zach knew the answer to that question.

"Back where he belongs."

CHAPTER 17

REVERSE WORLD

The audience gasped as the mirror spit Jak out onto the stage. He stood bewildered in the spotlight, dazed by the abrupt transition. A moment ago he had been fighting Zach's friends at the garbage dump, and now he was in the middle of *Snow White* at school, in front of a gawking audience.

"No!" he protested. "This wasn't supposed to go this way—"

"I'll say it wasn't!" Principal Ruggs said, looking

angrier than Jak had ever seen him. He grabbed Jak by the arm and dragged him away from the Magic Mirror before Jak could even try to get back to Zach's world. "I don't know how you pulled off that stunt with the mirror, or the quick change out of your costume, but you've turned this play into a joke quite enough!"

Jak had no idea what Ruggs was talking about. Glancing around, he saw Baron and Trina and Raquel scattered about the stage, grinning as though they had just gotten away with something. Ms. Fluke, dressed as the Wicked Queen, let out a sigh of relief.

"On with the show." She pointed her magic wand at the mirror and raised her voice dramatically. "Begone, cursed mirror! Trouble me no more!"

The tip of the wand flashed and—poof!—the magic mirror vanished in a billowing puff of black smoke. The audience cheered and applauded the spectacular effect even as Jak realized that he was cut off from Zach's world for good. There was no way to get back to all that magic!

"It's not fair," he groaned. "I was just getting started. . . ."

"You've done quite enough already!" Principal Ruggs insisted as he dragged Jak off the stage, where Raquel, Trina, and Baron were all taking bows as though they belonged there. Ms. Fluke grinned, obviously pleased by the audience's reaction. This was going to be a *Snow White* that nobody ever forgot.

"You don't understand—" Jak said.

"You bet I don't," the principal said, much less amused than the audience. "You've got a lot of explaining to do, young man. I've always gone easy on you before because of your unfortunate lack of magic, but that doesn't mean you can act up and do whatever you want, wherever you want!"

Jak didn't want to take the blame for whatever Zach had done. "But . . . but that wasn't me!"

"Of course it was. We all saw it with our own eyes," Ruggs said. "Don't make matters worse for yourself by trying to talk your way out of it. I want to see you and your parents in my office Monday morning. Do you hear me?"

Jak groaned. "Yes, sir!"

"Hang on!" Baron ran backstage, along with Trina and Raquel. "Don't be too hard on Jak. We were all in on it. We were just . . . *improvising* . . . to make the play funnier!"

"That's right," Trina said. "And it was all my idea!"

"No, it was my idea," Raquel insisted. "I talked Jak into it."

"It was a team effort," Baron said. "If you're going to punish Jak, you have to punish all of us."

Jak appreciated the other kids sticking up for him this way, even Raquel, who he barely knew. He suddenly realized that Sophie had been right before: giving up his real friends for a chance to be magic had been a selfish choice. No wonder everything had gone wrong for him on the other side of the mirror. He'd had the best friends in the world all along, and he'd turned his back on them just to be magic.

Big mistake, he thought.

Mr. Ruggs paused to listen to the applause coming from the audience. His stern expression softened into its usual good cheer.

"Well, I suppose there was no real harm done, except maybe to Ms. Fluke's nerves," he said, "and everyone seems to have enjoyed the show." He shrugged and let go of Jak's arm. "Just check with me before being so creative next time."

"Will do, Mr. R!" Jak said. "Trust me, I've learned my lesson."

He grinned at his friends, surprised at just how glad he was to see them again. He wasn't fibbing when he said he'd learned something important.

True friends came in handier than any magic!

OUR WORLD

Horace Greeley Middle School, read the sign above the front door. "Middle," *not* "Magic." Just the way it was supposed to be.

Zach beamed at the sign as he returned to his own school Monday morning. He went straight to his locker to make sure that Jak hadn't messed with his stuff while he was away. Zach confidently dialed the combo on the lock, tugged the door open—and a bucket of green slime spilled onto his head.

"What in the—?" he sputtered.

The plastic bucket bounced off his head onto the floor. Wiping the slime away from his eyes, he realized that the pail had been rigged to tip over onto him the moment he yanked the locker door open, but who had set this prank up?

Mocking laughter answered that question. He turned around to see Tricia—as opposed to Trina—recording his sticky calamity on her phone. She and her mean-girl posse were laughing and pointing at Zach as the slime oozed down him.

"Having a bad morning, Zach?" she taunted him. "Now we're *really* even!"

Tricia looked just as fashionably put together as he remembered. She sneered at him the way she always did. Scorn dripped from her voice.

Thank goodness!

She shrieked in dismay as Zach rushed forward and gave her a bear hug, smearing slime all over her.

"Just so you know," he told her, "you're actually pretty

cool when you're not trying so hard to be mean."

She blinked in surprise, unsure how to take that. For a moment, he glimpsed the real Tricia beneath the mean-girl act; then she realized everyone was watching them.

"OMG!" She shoved him away, but the slime was smeared all over her designer clothes. She raised her voice loud enough for the whole hallway to hear. "Gross! Have you lost your mind, Zach King?"

You can't fool me, he thought. *I know now that there's a nice person inside you somewhere. I know it!*

"What's going on here?" a stern voice bellowed.

Principal Riggs, bald as ever, his mustache bristling, stomped onto the scene. His face flushed and he shook his head as he spied Zach in the middle of the mess, dripping green onto the floor.

"Zach King!" he said in exasperation. "I might have known!"

"Good to see you, too, Mr. Riggs!" Zach said, meaning it.

Zach couldn't stop grinning. Tricia was up to no good and as mean as ever, Mr. Riggs was on the warpath, and

he was neck-deep in hot water as usual.

"That's detention for you, young man—again!"

Yep, everything was definitely back to normal!

Just the way Zach liked it.

TO BE CONTINUED....

KING TEAM

Zach

Beverly

I'm honored to work alongside such creative and hardworking team members. Thank you for your contributions to this magical story.
—Zach King

Andrew

Lukas

Mark

Kyle

A special thank-you to
Rachel King, David Linker, Cait Hoyt, Aaron Benitez, Sam Wickert,
Josie Stocks, and Sophia Johnson.

ABOUT THE AUTHOR

Zach King is a twenty-seven-year-old filmmaker who creates videos with a hint of "magic." With more than 25 million followers across his various social platforms, he is one of the hottest names in digital media. He's been featured on *Ellen* and on the red carpet at the Academy Awards—and he's partnered with Lego, Disney, and Kellogg's to create mind-blowing videos. In 2016, Zach and his wife competed in *The Amazing Race* along with other social media superstars. Born and raised in Portland, Oregon, Zach is the author of *Zach King: My Magical Life* and *Zach King: The Magical Mix-Up*. He lives with his family in Los Angeles.

More books by
ZACH KING!

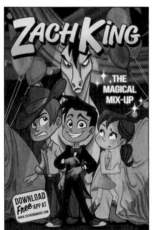

HARPER

An Imprint of HarperCollins*Publishers*

www.harpercollinschildrens.com • www.shelfstuff.com